HARPERCOLLI

Sto for

Year Olds

In the same series:

HARPERCOLLINS CHILDREN'S

Stories
for
7
Year Olds

Compiled by Julia Eccleshare

HarperCollins *Children's Books*

First published in the United Kingdom by HarperCollins, Young Lions, in 1992
Published in this revised edition by HarperCollins *Children's Books* in 2022
HarperCollins *Children's Books* is a division of HarperCollins*Publishers* Ltd
1 London Bridge Street
London SE1 9GF

www.harpercollins.co.uk

HarperCollins*Publishers*
Macken House, 39/40 Mayor Street Upper
Dublin 1, D01 C9W8, Ireland

2

ISBN 978-0-00-852473-9

A CIP catalogue record for this title is available from the British Library.

Typeset in 13/24pt ITC Century Std by
Palimpsest Book Production Ltd, Falkirk, Stirlingshire

Printed and bound in the UK using 100% renewable electricity
at CPI Group (UK) Ltd

MIX
Paper | Supporting
responsible forestry
FSC™ C007454

This book is produced from independently certified FSC™ paper
to ensure responsible forest management.

Find out more about HarperCollins and the environment at
www.harpercollins.co.uk/green

Contents

Mary Poppins: Laughing Gas

P. L. Travers
Illustrated by Mary Shephard

'Are you quite sure he will be at home?'
said Jane, as they got off the Bus, she
and Michael and Mary Poppins.

'Would my Uncle ask me to bring you to
tea if he intended to go out, I'd like to know?'
said Mary Poppins, who was evidently very

offended by the question. She was wearing her blue coat with the silver buttons and the blue hat to match, and on the days when she wore these it was the easiest thing in the world to offend her.

All three of them were on the way to pay a visit to Mary Poppins's uncle, Mr Wigg, and Jane and Michael had looked forward to the trip for so long that they were more than half afraid that Mr Wigg might not be in, after all.

'Why is he called Mr Wigg – does he wear one?' asked Michael, hurrying along beside Mary Poppins.

'He is called Mr Wigg because Mr Wigg is his name. And he doesn't wear one. He is bald,' said Mary Poppins. 'And if I have any more questions we will just go Back Home.' And she sniffed her usual sniff of displeasure.

Jane and Michael looked at each other and frowned. And the frown meant: 'Don't let's ask her anything else or we'll never get there.'

Mary Poppins put her hat straight at the Tobacconist's Shop at the corner. It had one of those curious windows where there seem to be three of you instead of one, so that if you look long enough at them you begin to feel you are not yourself but a whole crowd of somebody else. Mary Poppins sighed with pleasure, however, when she saw three of herself, each wearing a blue coat with silver buttons and a blue hat to match. She thought it was such a lovely sight that she wished there had been a dozen of her or even thirty. The more Mary Poppinses the better.

'Come along,' she said sternly, as though they had kept *her* waiting. Then they turned the corner and pulled the bell of Number Three, Robertson Road. Jane and Michael could hear it faintly echoing from a long way away and they knew that in one minute, or two at the most, they would be having tea with Mary Poppins's uncle, Mr Wigg, for the first time ever.

'If he's in, of course,' Jane said to Michael in a whisper. At that moment the door flew open and a thin, watery-looking lady appeared.

'Is he in?' said Michael quickly.

'I'll thank you,' said Mary Poppins, giving him a terrible glance, 'to let *me* do the talking.'

'How do you do, Mrs Wigg,' said Jane politely.

'Mrs Wigg!' said the thin lady, in a voice even thinner than herself. 'How dare you call me Mrs Wigg? No, thank you! I'm plain Miss

Persimmon *and* proud of it. Mrs Wigg indeed!' She seemed to be quite upset, and they thought Mr Wigg must be a very odd person if Miss Persimmon was so glad not to be Mrs Wigg.

'Straight up and first door on the landing,' said Miss Persimmon, and she went hurrying away down the passage saying: 'Mrs Wigg indeed!' to herself in a high, thin, outraged voice.

Jane and Michael followed Mary Poppins upstairs. Mary Poppins knocked at the door.

'Come in! Come in! And welcome!' called a loud, cheery voice from inside. Jane's heart was pitter-pattering with excitement.

'He *is* in!' she signalled to Michael with a look.

Mary Poppins opened the door and pushed

13

them in front of her. A large, cheerful room lay before them. At one end of it a fire was burning brightly and in the centre stood an enormous table laid for tea – four cups and saucers, piles of bread and butter, crumpets, coconut cakes and a large plum cake with pink icing.

'Well, this is indeed a Pleasure,' a huge voice greeted them, and Jane and Michael looked round for its owner. He was nowhere to be seen. The room appeared to be quite empty. Then they heard Mary Poppins saying crossly:

'Oh, Uncle Albert – not *again*? It's not your birthday, is it?'

And as she spoke she looked up at the ceiling. Jane and Michael looked up too and to their surprise saw a large, round man who was hanging in the air without holding on to anything. Indeed, he appeared to be *sitting* on the air, for his legs were crossed and he had just put down the newspaper which he had been reading when they came in.

'My dear,' said Mr Wigg, smiling down at the children, and looking apologetically at Mary Poppins, 'I'm very sorry, but I'm afraid it *is* my birthday.'

'Tch, tch, tch!' said Mary Poppins.

'I only remembered last night and there was no time then to send you a postcard asking you to come another day. Very distressing, isn't it?' he said, looking down at Jane and Michael.

'I can see you're rather surprised,' said Mr Wigg. And, indeed, their mouths were so wide open with astonishment that Mr Wigg, if he had been a little smaller, might almost have fallen into one of them.

'I'd better explain, I think,' Mr Wigg went on calmly. 'You see, it's this way. I'm a cheerful sort of man and very disposed to laughter. You wouldn't believe, either of you, the number of things that strike me as being funny. I can laugh at pretty nearly everything, I can.'

And with that Mr Wigg began to bob up and down, shaking with laughter at the thought of his own cheerfulness.

'Uncle Albert!' said Mary Poppins, and Mr Wigg stopped laughing with a jerk.

'Oh, beg pardon, my dear. Where was I? Oh, yes. Well, the funny thing about me is – all right, Mary, I won't laugh if I can help it! –

that whenever my birthday falls on a Friday, well, it's all up with me. Absolutely U.P.,' said Mr Wigg.

'But why—?' began Jane.

'But how—?' began Michael.

'Well, you see, if I laugh on that particular day I become so filled with Laughing Gas that I simply can't keep on the ground. Even if I smile it happens. The first funny thought, and I'm up like a balloon. And until I can think of something serious I can't get down again.' Mr Wigg began to chuckle at that, but he caught sight of Mary Poppins's face and stopped the chuckle, and continued: 'It's awkward, of course, but not unpleasant. Never happens to either of you, I suppose?'

Jane and Michael shook their heads.

'No, I thought not. It seems to be my own

special habit. Once, after I'd been to the Circus the night before, I laughed so much that – would you believe it? – I was up here for a whole twelve hours and couldn't get down till the last stroke of midnight. Then, of course, I came down with a flop because it was Saturday and not my birthday any more. It's rather odd, isn't it? Not to say funny?

'And now here it is Friday again and my birthday, and you two and Mary P. to visit me. Oh, Lordy, Lordy, don't make me laugh, I beg of you—'

But although Jane and Michael had done nothing very amusing, except to stare at him in astonishment, Mr Wigg began to laugh again loudly, and as he laughed he went bouncing and bobbing about in the air, with the newspaper rattling in his hand and his spectacles half on and half off his nose.

He looked so comic, floundering in the air like a great human bubble, clutching at the ceiling sometimes and sometimes at the gas bracket as he passed it, that Jane and Michael, though they were trying hard to be polite, just couldn't help doing what they did. They laughed. *And* they laughed. They shut their mouths tight to prevent the laughter escaping, but that didn't do any good. And presently they were rolling over and over on the floor, squealing and shrieking with laughter.

'Really!' said Mary Poppins. 'Really, *such* behaviour!'

'I can't help it, I can't help it!' shrieked

Michael, as he rolled into the fender. 'It's so terribly funny. Oh, Jane, *isn't* it funny?'

Jane did not reply, for a curious thing was happening to her. As she laughed she felt herself growing lighter and lighter, just as though she were being pumped full of air. It was a curious and delicious feeling and it made her want to laugh all the more. And then suddenly, with a bouncing bounce, she felt herself jumping through the air. Michael, to his astonishment, saw her go soaring up through the room. With a little bump her head touched the ceiling and then she went bouncing along it till she reached Mr Wigg.

'*Well!*' said Mr Wigg, looking very surprised indeed. 'Don't tell me it's *your* birthday, too?'

Jane shook her head.

'It's not? Then this Laughing Gas must be

catching! Hi – whoa there, look out for the mantelpiece!' This was to Michael, who had suddenly risen from the floor and was swooping through the air, roaring with laughter, and just grazing the china ornaments on the mantelpiece as he passed. He landed with a bounce right on Mr Wigg's knee.

'How do you do,' said Mr Wigg, heartily shaking Michael by the hand. 'I call this really friendly of you – bless my soul, I do! To come up to me since I couldn't come down to you – eh?' And then he and Michael looked at each other and flung back their heads and simply howled with laughter.

'I say,' said Mr Wigg to Jane, as he wiped his eyes. 'You'll be thinking I have the worst manners in the world. You're standing and you ought to be sitting – a nice young lady like you. I'm afraid I can't offer you a chair up here, but I think you'll find the air quite comfortable to sit on. I do.'

Jane tried it and found she could sit down quite comfortably on the air. She took off her hat and laid it down beside her and it hung there in space without any support at all.

'That's right,' said Mr Wigg. Then he turned and looked down at Mary Poppins.

'Well, Mary, we're fixed. And now I can enquire about *you*, my dear. I must say, I am very glad to welcome you and my two young friends here today – why, Mary, you're frowning. I'm afraid you don't approve of – er – all this.'

He waved his hand at Jane and Michael, and said hurriedly: 'I apologise, Mary, my dear. But you know how it is with me. Still, I must say I never thought my two young friends here would catch it, really I didn't, Mary! I suppose I should have asked them for another day or tried to think of something sad or something—'

'Well, I must say,' said Mary Poppins primly, 'that I have never in my life seen such a sight. And at your age, Uncle—'

'Mary Poppins, Mary Poppins, do come up!' interrupted Michael. 'Think of something funny and you'll find it's quite easy.'

'Ah, now do, Mary!' said Mr Wigg persuasively.

'We're lonely up here without you!' said Jane, and held out her arms towards Mary Poppins. '*Do* think of something funny!'

'Ah, *she* doesn't need to,' said Mr Wigg sighing. 'She can come up if she wants to, even without laughing – and she knows it.'

And he looked mysteriously and secretly at Mary Poppins as she stood down there on the hearth rug.

'Well,' said Mary Poppins, 'it's all very silly and undignified, but, since you're all up there and don't seem able to get down, I suppose I'd better come up, too.'

With that, to the surprise of Jane and Michael, she put her hands down at her sides and without a laugh, without even the faintest glimmer of a smile, she shot up through the air and sat down beside Jane.

'How many times, I should like to know,' she said snappily, 'have I told you to take off your coat when you come into a hot room?' And she unbuttoned Jane's coat and laid it neatly on the air beside the hat.

'That's right, Mary, that's right,' said Mr

Wigg contentedly, as he leant down and put his spectacles on the mantelpiece. 'Now we're all comfortable—'

'There's comfort *and* comfort,' sniffed Mary Poppins.

'And we can have tea,' Mr Wigg went on, apparently not noticing her remark. And then a startled look came over his face.

'My goodness!' he said. 'How dreadful! I've just realised – the table's down there and we're up here. What *are* we going to do? We're here and it's there. It's an awful tragedy – awful! But oh, it's terribly comic!' And he hid his face in his handkerchief and laughed loudly into it. Jane and Michael, though they did not want to miss the crumpets and the cakes, couldn't help laughing too, because Mr Wigg's mirth was so infectious.

Mr Wigg dried his eyes.

'There's only one thing for it,' he said. 'We must think of something serious. Something sad, very sad. And then we shall be able to get down. Now – one, two, three! Something *very* sad, mind you!'

They thought and thought, with their chins on their hands.

Michael thought of school, and that one day he would have to go there. But even that seemed funny today and he had to laugh.

Jane thought: *I shall be grown-up in another fourteen years*! But that didn't sound sad at all but quite nice and rather funny. She could not help smiling at the thought of herself grown-up, with long skirts and a handbag.

'There was my poor old Aunt Emily,' thought

Mr Wigg out loud. 'She was run over by an omnibus. Sad. Very sad.

Unbearably sad. Poor Aunt Emily. But they saved her umbrella. That was funny, wasn't it?' And before he knew where he was, he was heaving and trembling and bursting with laughter at the thought of Aunt Emily's umbrella.

'It's no good,' he said, blowing his nose. 'I give it up. And my young friends here seem to be no better at sadness than I am. Mary, can't *you* do something? We want our tea.'

To this day Jane and Michael cannot be sure of what happened then. All they know for certain is that, as soon as Mr Wigg had appealed to Mary Poppins, the table below began to wriggle on its legs. Presently it was swaying dangerously, and then with a rattle of china and with cakes lurching off their plates on to the cloth, the table came soaring through the room, gave one graceful turn, and landed beside them so that Mr Wigg was at its head.

'Good girl!' said Mr Wigg, smiling proudly upon her. 'I knew you'd fix something. Now, will you take the foot of the table and pour out, Mary? And the guests on either side of me. That's the idea,' he said, as Michael ran bobbing through the air and sat down on Mr Wigg's right. Jane was at his left hand. There they were, all together, up in the air and the table between them. Not a single piece of bread and butter or a lump of sugar had been left behind.

Mr Wigg smiled contentedly.

'It is usual, I think, to begin with bread and butter,' he said to Jane and Michael, 'but as it's

my birthday we will begin the wrong way –
which I always think is the *right* way – with
the Cake!'

And he cut a large slice for everybody.

'More tea?' he said to Jane. But before she
had time to reply there was a quick, sharp
knock at the door.

'Come in!' called Mr Wigg.

The door opened, and there stood Miss
Persimmon with a jug of hot water on a
tray.

'I thought, Mr Wigg,' she began, looking
searchingly round the room, 'you'd be wanting
some more hot—Well, I never! I simply
never!' she said, as she caught sight of them
all seated on the air round the table. 'Such
goings on I never did see! In all my born days
I never saw such. I'm sure, Mr Wigg, I always

knew *you* were a bit odd. But I've closed my eyes to it – being as how you paid your rent regular. But such behaviour as this – having tea in the air with your guests – Mr Wigg, sir, I'm astonished at you! It's that undignified, and for a gentleman of your age – I never did—'

'But perhaps you will, Miss Persimmon!' said Michael.

'Will what?' said Miss Persimmon haughtily.

'Catch the Laughing Gas, as we did,' said Michael.

Miss Persimmon flung back her head scornfully.

'I hope, young man,' she retorted, 'I have more respect for myself than to go bouncing about in the air like a rubber ball on the end of a bat. I'll stay on my own feet, thank you, or my name's not Amy Persimmon, and – oh dear, oh *dear*, my goodness, oh *DEAR* – what *is* the matter? I can't walk, I'm going, I – oh, help, *HELP!*'

For Miss Persimmon, quite against her will, was off the ground and was stumbling through the air, rolling from side to side like a very thin barrel, balancing the tray in her hand. She was almost weeping with distress as she arrived at the table and put down her jug of hot water.

'Thank you,' said Mary Poppins in a calm, very polite voice.

Then Miss Persimmon turned and went wafting down again, murmuring as she went: 'So undignified – and me a well-behaved, steady-going woman. I must see a doctor— '

When she touched the floor she ran

hurriedly out of the room, wringing her hands, and not giving a single glance backwards.

'So undignified!' they heard her moaning as she shut the door behind her.

'Her name can't be Amy Persimmon, because she *didn't* stay on her own feet!' whispered Jane to Michael.

But Mr Wigg was looking at Mary Poppins – a curious look, half-amused, half-accusing.

'Mary, Mary, you shouldn't – bless my soul, you shouldn't, Mary. The poor old body will never get over it. But, oh, my goodness, didn't she look funny waddling through the air – my gracious goodness, but didn't she?'

And he and Jane and Michael were off again, rolling about the air, clutching their sides and gasping with laughter at the thought of how funny Miss Persimmon had looked.

'Oh dear!' said Michael. 'Don't make me laugh any more. I can't stand it. I shall break!'

'Oh, oh, oh!' cried Jane, as she gasped for breath, with her hand over her heart.

'Oh, my Gracious, Glorious, Galumphing Goodness!' roared Mr Wigg, dabbing his eyes with his coat-tail because he couldn't find his handkerchief.

'IT IS TIME TO GO HOME.' Mary Poppins's voice sounded above the roars of laughter like a trumpet.

And suddenly, with a rush, Jane and Michael and Mr Wigg came down. They landed on the floor with a huge bump, all together. The thought that they would have to go home was the first sad thought of the afternoon, and the moment it was in their minds the Laughing Gas went out of them.

Jane and Michael sighed as they watched Mary Poppins come slowly down the air, carrying Jane's coat and hat.

Mr Wigg sighed, too. A great, long, heavy sigh.

'Well, isn't that a pity?' he said soberly. 'It's very sad that you've got to go home. I never enjoyed an afternoon so much – did you?'

'Never,' said Michael sadly, feeling how dull it was to be down on the earth again with no Laughing Gas inside him.

'Never, never,' said Jane, as she stood on tiptoe and kissed Mr Wigg's withered-apple cheeks. 'Never, never, never, never . . . !'

They sat on either side of Mary Poppins going home on the bus. They were both very quiet, thinking over the lovely afternoon. Presently Michael said sleepily to Mary Poppins: 'How often does your Uncle get like that?'

'Like what?' said Mary Poppins sharply, as though Michael had deliberately said something to offend her.

'Well – all bouncy and boundy and laughing and going up in the air.'

'Up in the air?' Mary Poppins's voice was high and angry. 'What do you mean, pray, up in the air?'

Jane tried to explain.

'Michael means – is your Uncle often full of Laughing Gas, and does he often go rolling and bobbing about on the ceiling when—'

'Rolling and bobbing! What an idea! Rolling and bobbing on the ceiling! You'll be telling me next he's a balloon!' Mary Poppins gave an offended sniff.

'But he did!' said Michael. 'We saw him.'

'What, roll and bob? How dare you! I'll have you know that my Uncle is a sober, honest, hard-working man, and you'll be kind enough to speak of him respectfully. And don't bite your Bus ticket! Roll and bob, indeed – the idea!'

Michael and Jane looked across Mary Poppins at each other. They said nothing, for they had learnt that it was better not to argue with Mary Poppins, no matter how odd anything seemed.

But the look that passed between them said: 'Is it true or isn't it? About Mr Wigg. Is Mary Poppins right, or are we?'

But there was nobody to give them the right answer.

The Bus roared on, wildly lurching and bounding.

Mary Poppins sat between them, offended and silent, and presently, because they were very tired, they crept closer to her and leant up against her sides and fell asleep, still wondering . . .

Dolphin Boy

Michael Morpurgo
Illustrated by Penny Bell

Once upon a time, the little fishing village was a happy place. Not any more.

Once upon a time, the fishermen of the village used to go out fishing every day. Not any more.

Once upon a time, there were lots of fish to catch. Not any more.

Now the boats lay high and dry on the beach, their paint peeling in the sun, their sails rotting in the rain.

Jim's father was the only fisherman who still took his boat out. That was because he loved the *Sally May* like an old friend and just couldn't bear to be parted from her.

Whenever Jim wasn't at school, his father would take him along. Jim loved the *Sally May* as much as his father did in spite of her raggedy old sails. There was nothing he liked better than taking the helm, or hauling in the nets with his father.

One day, on his way home from school, Jim saw his father sitting alone on the quay, staring out at an empty bay. Jim couldn't see the *Sally May* anywhere. 'Where's the *Sally May*?' he asked.

'She's up on the beach,' said his father, 'with all the other boats. I've caught no fish at all for a week, Jim. She needs new sails and I haven't got the money to pay for them. No fish, no money. We can't live without money. I'm sorry, Jim.'

That night Jim cried himself to sleep.

After that, Jim always took the beach road to school because he liked to have a look at the *Sally May* before school began.

He was walking along the beach one morning when he saw something lying in the sand amongst the seaweed. It looked like a big log at first, but it wasn't. It was moving. It had a tail and a head. It was a dolphin!

Jim knelt in the sand beside him. The boy

and the dolphin looked into each other's eyes. Jim knew then exactly what he had to do.

'Don't worry,' he said. 'I'll fetch help. I'll be back soon, I promise.'

He ran all the way up the hill to school as fast as he could go. Everyone was in the playground.

'You've got to come!' he cried. 'There's a dolphin on the beach! We've got to get him back in the water or he'll die.'

Down the hill to the beach the children ran, the teachers as well. Soon everyone in the village was there – Jim's father and his mother too.

'Fetch the *Sally May's* sail!' cried Jim's mother. 'We'll roll him on to it.'

When they had fetched the sail, Jim crouched down beside the dolphin's head, stroking him and comforting him. 'Don't worry,' he whispered. 'We'll soon have you back in the sea.'

They spread out the sail and rolled him on to it very gently. Then, when everyone had taken a tight grip of the sail, Jim's father gave the word, 'Lift!'

With a hundred hands lifting together, they soon carried the dolphin down to the sea where they laid him in the shallows and let the waves wash over him.

The dolphin squeaked and clicked and slapped the sea with his smiley mouth. He was swimming now, but he didn't seem to want to leave. He swam round and round.

'Off you go,' Jim shouted, wading in and trying to push him out to sea. 'Off you go.' And off he went at last.

Everyone was clapping and cheering and waving goodbye. Jim just wanted him to come back again. But he didn't. Along with everyone else, Jim stayed and watched until he couldn't see him any more.

That day at school Jim could think of nothing but the dolphin. He even thought up a name for him. 'Smiler' seemed to suit him perfectly.

The moment school was over, Jim ran back to the beach hoping and praying Smiler might have come back. But Smiler wasn't there. He was nowhere to be seen.

Filled with sudden sadness he rushed down to the pier. 'Come back, Smiler!' he cried. 'Please come back. Please!'

At that very moment, Smiler rose up out of the sea right in front of him! He turned over and over in the air before he crashed down into the water, splashing Jim from head to toe.

Jim didn't think twice. He dropped his bag, pulled off his shoes and dived off the pier.

At once Smiler was there beside him – swimming all around him, leaping over him, diving under him. Suddenly Jim found himself being lifted up from below. He was sitting on Smiler! He was riding him!

Off they sped out to sea, Jim clinging on as best he could. Whenever he fell off – and he often did – Smiler was always there, so that Jim could always get on again. The further they went, the faster they went. And the faster they went, the more Jim liked it.

Round and round the bay Smiler took him, and then back at last to the quay. By this time everyone in the village had seen them and the children were diving off the quay and swimming out to meet them.

All of them wanted to swim with Smiler, to touch him, to stroke him, to play with him. And Smiler was happy to let them. They were having the best time of their lives.

Every day after that, Smiler would be swimming near the quay waiting for Jim, to give him his ride. And every day the children swam with him and played with him too. They loved his kind eyes and smiling face.

Smiler was everyone's best friend.

Then one day, Smiler wasn't there. They waited for him. They looked for him. But he never came. The next day he wasn't there either, nor the next, nor the next.

Jim was broken-hearted, and so were all

the children. Everyone in the village missed Smiler, young and old alike, and longed for him to come back. Each day they looked and each day he wasn't there.

When Jim's birthday came, his mother gave him something she hoped might cheer him up – a wonderful carving of a dolphin – she'd made it herself out of driftwood. But not even that seemed to make Jim happy.

Then his father had a bright idea. 'Jim,' he said, 'why don't we all go out in the *Sally May*? Would you like that?'

'Yes!' Jim cried. 'Then we could look for Smiler too.'

So they hauled the *Sally May* down to the water and set the sails. Out of the bay they went, out on to the open sea where, despite her raggedy old sails, the *Sally May* flew along over the waves. Jim loved the wind in his face, and the salt spray on his lips. There were lots of gulls and gannets, but no sight of Smiler anywhere. He called for him again and again, but he didn't come.

The sun was setting by now, the sea glowing gold around them.

'I think we'd better be getting back,' Jim's father told him.

'Not yet,' Jim cried. 'He's out here somewhere. I know he is.'

As the *Sally May* turned for home, Jim called out one last time, 'Come back, Smiler! Please come back. Please!'

Suddenly the sea began to boil and bubble around the boat, almost as if it was coming alive. And it WAS alive too, alive with dolphins! There seemed to be hundreds of them, leaping out of the sea alongside them, behind them, in front of them.

Then, one of them leapt clear over the *Sally May*, right above Jim's head. It was Smiler!

Smiler had come back, and by the look of it he'd brought his whole family with him.

As the *Sally May* sailed into the bay everyone saw her coming, the dolphins dancing all about her in the golden sea. What a sight it was!

Within days the village was full of visitors, all of them there to see the famous dolphins and to see Smiler playing with Jim and the children.

And every morning, the *Sally May* and all the little fishing boats put to sea crammed with visitors, all of them only too happy to pay for their trip of a lifetime. They loved every minute of it, holding on to their hats and laughing with delight as the dolphins frisked and frolicked around them.

Jim had never been so happy in all his life. He had Smiler back, and now his father had all the money he needed to buy new sails for the *Sally May*. And all the other fishermen too could mend their sails and paint their boats. Once again, the village was a happy place.

As for the children . . .

. . . they could go swimming with the dolphins whenever they wanted to. They could stroke them, and swim with them and play with them, and even talk to them. But they all knew that only one dolphin would ever let anyone sit on him.

That was Smiler.

And they all knew that there was only one

person in the whole world who Smiler would take for a ride.

And that was Jim.

The Great Mushroom Mistake

Penelope Lively
Illustrated by Ruthine Burton

Birthday presents for mothers can be a problem. In the first place there is the expense. Obviously diamond necklaces and holidays in Bermuda are out of the question, even if your mother is the sort of person who would fancy such things. In the second place there is the difficult matter of choice. A present should be just what the person wants; to know what this might be you have to make a study of the person in question.

Sue and Alan Hancock had studied their mother as much as most children. That is to say, they knew warning signs of ill temper (a generally frowsty appearance, a tendency to say no in reply to any request) and signs of a good mood when almost anything might be allowed (humming while making the beds, preparation of large meals). And they could hardly help knowing what she was interested in.

Mrs Hancock was good at growing things. The Hancocks' garden did not just bloom: it crackled and exploded and positively burst out with leaf and petal. Mrs Hancock had green fingers, to put it simply. Everything she planted came popping out of the ground and then shot outwards and upwards; her roses and her peas were the envy of the neighbour-hood. Whenever she had a spare minute she was out in the garden. Indeed, when the children were small they had been vaguely under the impression that their mother could not stand up straight, because their most usual view of her was of someone bent double like a clothes peg, peering down at her seedling plants, or scraping and scratching at the soil.

And so birthday presents were not really a problem. There were new trowels and new gardening gloves and special plants and hanks of new twine. But this year they wanted something special – something different, something no one else's mother had. They searched the usual shops, and were not satisfied. Indeed, it was not until the very day before the birthday that they walked past the greengrocer on the corner near their school and saw the very thing.

Outside the shop were two shallow wooden boxes from which bubbled a profusion of gleaming white mushrooms: crisp fresh delicious-looking mushrooms. And alongside the boxes was a notice: GROW YOUR OWN MUSHROOMS! A NEW CROP EVERY DAY!

They looked at each other. Their mother had grown just about everything in her time, but never mushrooms. They went into the shop. They bought a small plastic bag labelled MUSHROOM SPORE, another bag of earthy stuff in which you were supposed to plant it, and an instruction leaflet.

Mrs Hancock was thrilled. She couldn't wait to get going. The instruction leaflet said that the mushrooms liked to grow indoors in a darkish place. A cellar would do nicely, it said, or the cupboard under the stairs. The Hancocks had no cellar and the cupboard under the stairs was full of the sort of things that takes refuge in cupboards under the stairs: old shoes and suitcases and a broken tennis racket and a chair with only three legs. Mrs Hancock decided that the only place was the cupboard in the spare room, which was used by guests only – and no guest was threatening for some while. The children helped her to spread the earthy stuff out in boxes and scatter the spores. Then, apparently, all they had to do was wait.

During the night, Alan woke once and

thought he heard a faint creaking sound, like a tree straining in the wind. And when, in the morning, they opened the door of the spare-room cupboard there in the boxes was a fine growth of mushrooms – fat adult mushrooms and baby mushrooms pushing up under and around them. Mrs Hancock was delighted; the children preened themselves on the success of their present; everyone had fried mushrooms for breakfast.

The next day they found the cupboard door half open and mushrooms tumbling out on to the floor. 'Gracious!' said Mrs Hancock. 'It'll be mushroom soup for lunch today.' The instruction leaflet said DO NOT SOW MORE SPORES TILL CROPPING CEASES, so they decided to wait and see what happened. The next day there were as many mushrooms again. They had mushrooms for every meal.

On the third day there were not only mushrooms bursting from the cupboard but a small clutch under the washbasin. There were far too many to eat; Mrs Hancock gave some to the postman and the milkman and the people next door.

That night, the creaking was more definite. Both children heard it; a sound something between a rustling and a splitting – the sound of growth. And in the morning there were mushrooms all over the spare-room floor, a clump on the stairs and several clusters under the table in the hall. The Hancocks gazed at them in astonishment. 'They *are* doing well,' said Mrs Hancock, with a slight trace of anxiety in her voice. It took some time to collect them all up, and the people next door said thanks very much but they couldn't really do with any more. The children were getting heartily tired of mushroom soup. In the end they had to throw a lot away.

Over the next few days, the mushroom invasion continued. They found mushrooms in the bathroom and beside the cooker and in the toy chest. When they got up in the mornings they had to walk downstairs on a carpet of small mushrooms which squeaked faintly underfoot, like colonies of mice. It was when Mrs Hancock had to vacuum mushrooms from the sitting-room carpet that they realised the situation had got quite out of control. 'Stop planting the things,' said Mr Hancock. 'I have,' wailed Mrs Hancock. 'I

only ever did plant them the once. They just keep coming.'

'Green fingers,' said her husband sourly. 'That's the trouble.' Everyone looked despairingly at Mrs Hancock's hands: perfectly ordinary sensible-looking hands but clearly, in this instance, fatal.

They filled the dustbins with mushrooms. They took plastic sacks of mushrooms to the town dump. And still they came, bubbling up every night, springing cheerfully from window ledges and skirting boards and behind pictures. The house smelled of mushroom: a clean, earthy smell.

Mrs Hancock called in the Pest Control Service, a business-like man with a van who took one look at the mushrooms and shook his head in perplexity. 'I've never seen anything like it,' he said. 'Now if it was rats or cockroaches I'd know where I was. Or wasps. Or ants. This is phenomenal.' He looked out of the window at the garden, and then at Mrs Hancock; 'I'd say you had a way with nature, madam. Ever thought of going into the wholesale business?' He left a can of weedkiller and said he would come back in a few days. Mrs Hancock mopped the whole house out with weedkiller. The next morning, the night's growth of mushrooms looked a little sickly, like someone who has had a late night and a touch of indigestion, but the day after they were as thriving as ever, coming up here, there and everywhere so that the floors of every room looked softly cobbled. The children were sent out to buy yet more black plastic sacks.

The Pest Control man shook his head

again. 'They've got a hold,' he said. 'That's what. Frankly, I don't know what to suggest. It's interesting, mind. I wouldn't let the papers get on to it – you could find yourself on the front page.' The Hancocks stared at him coldly. 'I'll have a think,' he said, going out of the front door. 'The great thing is, don't panic.'

That evening, Mrs Hancock said, 'There's nothing for it. We're going to have to call in Aunt Sadie.' There was a silence; Mr Hancock sighed. 'A desperate measure,' he said. 'But I see your point.'

Many families have an Aunt Sadie: an expert all-purpose undefeatable long-distance interferer. The relation who scents defects as soon as she has one foot inside the door – 'Pity that paint turned out the wrong colour',

'I see Sue's hair's still growing dead straight',
'I'm wondering if Alan's teeth don't need a
brace'. Aunt Sadie could kill any occasion
stone dead: Christmas, birthdays, family
outings. Strong men fled at the sight of Aunt
Sadie. And there was nothing Aunt Sadie
enjoyed more than muscling in on a situation
(preferably uninvited) and, as she called it
'lending a willing hand'. What chance, Mr
Hancock agreed, would a few mushrooms have
against Aunt Sadie?

Aunt Sadie, dropping her suitcase in the
hall, stalked through the house inspecting.
She peered at the mushrooms, and the
mushrooms, just starting on their second
crop of the day, peeped back from cracks in
the floorboards and sidled out from under
the carpets. She fetched the dustpan and

shovelled out a couple of pounds of them from inside the grandfather clock, where they had been surging up unnoticed for several days. The Hancocks watched with interest. Aunt Sadie, in her time, had reduced a six-foot traffic warden to tears and disrupted an entire police station. She went upstairs and could be heard tramping around. When she came down Mr Hancock said, 'Well, Sadie – bit out of your line, eh?' This, of course, was meant to provoke, and it did.

Aunt Sadie glared at him. 'I'll want a free hand. I'll want everyone out of the way except the children. You'd better take Mary for a short holiday.'

'But I don't want a holiday . . .' Mrs Hancock began.

'You'll have to. There's no two ways about

it. It's having you here that's encouraged the things. I always said all that gardening was unnatural.' She rolled up her sleeves.

'What do you want *us* for?' asked Sue.

'Labour force,' snapped Aunt Sadie.

The next few days were pandemonium. 'There's nothing,' said Aunt Sadie decisively, 'that a good spring-clean won't deal with.' Carpets, curtains, chairs and tables were hurled hither and thither. The house looked as though a bomb had hit it. The children scurried to and fro with buckets and scrubbing brushes.

The mushrooms grew, undaunted.

The children were sent shopping. 'Ten gallons of disinfectant!' said the manager of the hardware shop. 'Jeyes Fluid *and* ammonia *and* a quart of insecticide! You people in some kind of trouble?'

Aunt Sadie, with the children panting behind her, scrubbed and sprayed and swabbed. For five days she and the mushrooms did battle. A dose of Jeyes Fluid had them coming up blackened but valiantly fighting back. Insecticide and flea powder sent them reeling for a couple of days. 'We've got them on the run!' said Aunt Sadie grimly, but then a new wave broke out from the airing cupboard. The war was on again.

All this had quite distracted Aunt Sadie from her usual occupation when visiting: general interference. In the normal way of things she would have been busy suggesting that everything the family did should be done differently and in particular that the children were a total disaster in terms of appearance, behaviour and anything else you like to mention. Their health, especially, was of intense interest: they were spotty, she would announce, or pasty-looking, or too large or too small or too fat or too thin, and various appalling tonics and potions were produced to set matters right.

With relief, Sue and Alan realised that on this occasion she was far too taken up with the mushrooms to pay them much attention at all. Until one evening Alan made the mistake of coughing.

'You've got a cough,' said Aunt Sadie, instantly alert.

'Bit of biscuit got stuck,' said Alan hastily.

'I know a chronic cough when I hear one,' said Aunt Sadie, grim. She reached into the enormous handbag that accompanied her even into the bathroom. Out came a bottle of fearsome-looking brown stuff, and a spoon. 'Open your mouth.'

Whether what happened next was an accident or not will never be known. As the first horrific whiff of the cough mixture reached Alan's nose he gave a kind of convulsive snort. The cough mixture blew from the spoon, the spoon flew from Aunt Sadie's hand, Aunt Sadie with a cry of annoyance leaned forward to rescue it and knocked over the open bottle upon the table, which lurched to the floor gushing thick brown cough mixture in all directions. Everyone began to blame everyone else until suddenly Sue cried, 'Look!'

The advancing tide of cough mixture had reached a clump of mushrooms that had sprung up unnoticed from the skirting board.

And as it did so a very curious thing happened. The mushrooms vanished. They simply expired. One moment they were there and the next there was nothing but a little heap of dust and a puddle of cough mixture.

'Well!' said Aunt Sadie, staring, 'That's interesting . . .'

'If it does that to people too,' said Alan, 'it's a jolly good thing I didn't swallow it.'

Aunt Sadie ignored him, 'I think,' she said thoughtfully, 'we may be on to something.'

This time Aunt Sadie did the shopping herself. It is not just anyone who can persuade a chemist to make up several gallons of cough mixture, and supply it in a large can with a spray attachment. What the chemist said or thought is not known; Aunt Sadie had a way of discouraging unwelcome curiosity. Anyway, she returned, armed with the new weapon, and set to work. And within a matter of hours there was not a mushroom in sight, nor did any appear the next morning, nor the next. Aunt Sadie stalked around the house in triumph, and sent for Mr and Mrs Hancock. The children, eyeing the remains of the cough mixture with awe, were quite extraordinarily careful not to cough.

And that was the end of the great mushroom mistake. For her next birthday the children gave their mother six handkerchiefs and some talcum powder, an unadventurous present but a safe one. And Aunt Sadie's reputation soared to even greater heights; there was nothing, it was generally agreed, with which she could not deal. The government, Mr Hancock suggested, would do well to hire her and keep her in hand for use in case of riots, epidemics, earthquake or flood. And the Pest Control man, who happened to call back the day before Aunt Sadie left, is still trying to get the recipe for that cough mixture from her.

Vasilissa, Baba Yaga
and the Little Doll

Retold by Naomi Lewis
Illustrated by Rachael Saunders

In a far-off land in a far-off time, on the edge of a great forest, lived a girl named Vasilissa. Ah, poor Vasilissa! She was no more than eight years old when her mother died. But she had a friend, and that one was better than most.

Who was this friend? A doll. As the mother lay ill she had called the child to her bedside. 'Vasilissa,' she said, 'here is a little doll. Take good care of her, and whenever you are in great need, give her some food and ask for her help; she will tell you what to do. Take her, with my blessing; but remember, she is your secret; no one else must know of her at all. Now I can die content.'

The father of Vasilissa grieved for a time, then married a new wife, thinking that she would care for the little girl. But did she indeed! She had two daughters of her own, and not one of the three had a grain of love for Vasilissa. From early dawn to the last light of day, in the hot sun or the icy wind, they kept her toiling at all the hardest tasks, in or out of the house; never did she have a word of thanks. Yet whatever they set her to do was done, and done in time. For when she truly needed help she would set her doll on a ledge or table, give her a little food and drink, and tell the doll her troubles. With her help all was done.

One day in the late autumn the father had to leave for the town, a journey of many days. He set off at earliest dawn.

Darkness fell early. Rain beat on the cottage windows; the wind howled down the chimney – just the time for the wife to work a plan she had in mind. To each of the girls she gave a task: the first was set to making lace, the second to knitting stockings, Vasilissa to spinning.

'No stirring from your place, my girls, before you have done,' said the woman. Then, leaving them a single candle, she went to bed.

The three worked on for a while, but the light was small, and flickered. One sister pretended to trim the wick and it went out altogether – just as the mother had planned.

'Now we're in trouble,' said the girl. 'For where's the new light to come from?'

'There's only one place,' said her sister, 'and that's from Baba Yaga.'

'That's right,' said the other. 'But who's to go?

My needles shine;
The job's not mine.'

'I can manage too,' said the other.

'My lace-pins shine;
the job's not mine.

Vasilissa must go.'

'Yes, Vasilissa must go!' they cried together. And they pushed her out of the door.

Now who was Baba Yaga? She was a mighty witch; her hut was set on claws, like the legs of giant hens. She rode in a mortar over the highest mountains, speeding it on with the pestle, sweeping away her traces with a broom. And she would crunch up in a trice any human who crossed her path.

But Vasilissa had a friend, and that one better than most. She took the doll from her pocket, and set some bread before her. 'Little doll,' she said, 'they are sending me into the forest to fetch a light from Baba Yaga's hut – and who has ever returned from there? Help me, little doll.'

The doll ate, and her eyes grew bright as

stars. 'Have no fear,' said she. 'While I am with you nothing can do you harm. But remember – no one else must know of your secret. Now let us start.'

How dark it was in the forest of towering trees! How the leaves hissed, how the branches creaked and moaned in the wind! But Vasilissa walked resolutely on, hour after hour. Suddenly, the earth began to tremble and a horseman thundered by. Both horse and rider were glittering white, hair and mane, swirling cloak and bridle too; and as they passed, the sky showed the first white light of dawn.

Vasilissa journeyed on, then again she heard a thundering noise, and a second horse and rider flashed into sight. Both shone red as scarlet, red as flame, swirling cloak and bridle too; as they rode beyond her view, the sun rose high. It was day.

On she walked, on and on, until she reached a clearing in the woods. In the centre was a hut – but the hut had feet; and they were the claws of hens. It was Baba Yaga's home, no doubt about that. All around was a fence of bones, and the posts were topped with skulls: a fearful sight in the fading light! And as she gazed, a third horseman thundered past; but this time horse and rider were black and black, swirling cloak and bridle too. They vanished into the gloom, and it was night. But, as darkness fell, the eyes of the skulls lit up like lamps and everything in the glade could be seen as sharp as day.

Swish! Swoosh! Varoom! Varoom! As Vasilissa stood there, frozen stiff with fear, a terrible noise came from over the forest. The wind screeched, the leaves hissed – Baba Yaga was riding home in her huge mortar, using her pestle as an oar, sweeping away the traces with her broom. At the gate of the hut she stopped, and sniffed the air with her long nose.

'Phoo! Phoo! I smell Russian flesh!' she croaked. 'Who's there? Out you come!'

Vasilissa took courage, stepped forward and made a low curtsey.

'It is I, Vasilissa. My sisters sent me for a light, since ours went out.'

'Oh, so that's it!' said the witch. 'I know those girls, and their mother, too. Well, nothing's for nothing, as they say; you must work for me for a while, then we'll see about the light.' She turned to the hut and sang in a high shrill screech:

'Open gates! Open gates!
Baba Yaga waits.'

The weird fence opened; the witch seized the girl's arm in her bony fingers and pushed her into the hut. 'Now,' she said, 'get a light from the lamps outside,' – she meant the skulls – 'and serve my supper. It's in the oven, and the soup's in the cauldron there.' She lay down on a bench while Vasilissa carried the food to the table until she was quite worn out, but she dared not stop. And the witch devoured much more than ten strong men could have eaten – whole geese and hens and roasted pigs; loaf after loaf; huge buckets of beer and wine, cider and Russian kvass. At last, all that remained was a crust of bread.

'There's your supper, girl,' said the witch. 'But

you must earn it, mind; I don't like greed. While I'm off tomorrow you must clear out the yard; it hasn't been touched for years, and it quite blocks out the view. Then you must sweep the hut, wash the linen, cook the dinner – and mind you cook enough; I was half-starved tonight. Then – for I'll have no lazybones around – there's another little job. You see that sack? It's full of black beans, wheat and poppy seed, some other things too, I dare say. Sort them out into their separate lots, and if a single one is out of place, woe betide! Into the cauldron you shall go, and I'll eat you up for breakfast in a trice.'

So saying, she lay down by the stove and was instantly fast asleep. *Sno-o-o-re* . . . *Sno-o-o-re* . . . It was a horrible sound.

Vasilissa took the doll from her pocket and gave her the piece of bread. 'Little doll,' said she. 'How am I to do all these tasks? Or even one of them? How can a little doll like you help now? We are lost indeed.'

'Vasilissa,' said the doll. 'Again I tell you, have no fear. Say your prayers and go to sleep. Tomorrow knows what is hidden from yesterday.'

She slept – but she woke early, before the first glimmer of day. Where should she start on the mountain of work? Then she heard a thundering of hoofs; white horse and white rider flashed past the window – suddenly it was dawn. The light in the skulls' eyes dwindled and went out. Then the poor girl hid in the shadows, for she saw Baba Yaga get to her feet – *Creak! Creak!* – and shuffle to the door. There, the witch gave a piercing whistle, and mortar, pestle and broom came hurtling towards her, stopping where she stood. In she stepped, off she rode, over treetops, through the clouds, using the pestle like an oar, sweeping away her traces with the broom. Just as she soared away, the red horse and red rider thundered past: suddenly it was day, and the sun shone down.

Vasilissa turned away from the window, but what was this? She could not believe her eyes.

Every task was done. The yard was cleared, the linen washed, the grains and the seeds were all in separate bins, the dinner was set to cook. And there was the little doll, waiting to get back in her pocket. 'All you need to do,' said the doll, 'is to lay the table and serve it all, hot and hot, when she returns. But keep your wits about you all the same, for she's a sly one.'

The winter daylight faded fast; again there

was a thundering of hoofs; black horse, black rider sped through the glade and were gone. Darkness fell, and the eyes of the skulls once more began to glow. And then, with a swish and a roar, down swept the mortar, out stepped Baba Yaga.

'Well, girl, why are you standing idle? You know what I told you.'

'The work is all done, Baba Yaga.'

Baba Yaga looked and looked, but done it all was. So she sat down, grumbling and mumbling, to eat her supper. It was good, very good: it put her in a pleasant humour, for a witch.

'Tell me, girl, why do you sit there as if you were dumb?'

'Baba Yaga, I did not dare to speak – but, now, if you permit it, may I ask a question?'

'Ask if you will, but remember that not

every question leads to good. The more you know, the older you grow.'

'Well, Baba Yaga, can you tell me, who is the white rider on the white horse, the one who passed at dawn?'

'He is my Bright Morning, and he brings the earliest light.'

'Then who is the rider all in red on the flame-red horse?'

'Ah, he is my Fiery Sun and brings the day.'

'And who is the horseman all in black on the coal-black horse?'

'He is my Dark Night. All are my faithful servants. Now I shall ask *you* a question; mind you answer me properly. How did you do all those tasks I set you?'

Vasilissa recalled her mother's words, never to tell the secret of the doll.

'My mother gave me a blessing before she died, and that helps me when in need.'

'A blessing! I want no blessed children here! Out you get! Away! Away!' And she pushed her through the door. 'You've earned your pay – now take it.' She took down one of the gatepost skulls, fixed it on a stick, and thrust it into Vasilissa's hand. 'Now – off!'

Vasilissa needed no second bidding. She hastened on, her path now lit by the eyes of the fearful lamp. And so, at last, she was home.

'Why have you taken so long?' screamed the mother and the sisters. They had been in darkness ever since she left. They had gone in every direction to borrow a light, but once it was inside in the house, every flame went out. So they seized the skull with joy.

But the glaring eyes stared back; wherever

they turned they could not escape the scorching rays. Soon, all that remained of the three was a little ash. Then the light of the skull went out for ever; its task was done.

Vasilissa buried it in the garden, and a bush of red roses sprang up on the spot. She did not fear to be alone, for the little doll kept her company. And when her father returned, rejoicing to see her, this tale she told him, just as it has been told to you.

The Lory Who Longed for Honey

Leila Berg
Illustrated by Ruthine Burton

Once upon a time, in a hot sunny country, lived a very bright and beautiful parrot. He was red and green and gold and blue, with a dark purple top to his head. His real name was Lory. And he lived on honey.

There were hundreds of flowers growing among the trees, so all he had to do when he was hungry was to fly down and lick the honey out of the flowers. As a matter of fact, he had a tongue that was specially shaped for getting honey out of flowers. So he always had plenty to eat, and managed very well. All day long he flew about in the hot sunshine, while the monkeys chattered and the bright birds screamed. And as long as he had plenty of honey, he was perfectly happy.

Then one day a sailor came to the forest looking for parrots. He found the parrot that liked honey and took him away. He didn't know that this parrot's real name was a Lory. He didn't know that he had a tongue specially shaped for getting honey out of flowers. He didn't even know he liked honey. He only knew he was a very bright and beautiful parrot and he meant to take him to England and sell him. So on board the ship he fed the parrot on sunflower seeds and taught him to say: 'What have you got, what have you got, what have you got for me?' And whenever the Lory said this, the sailor gave him a sunflower seed. Although, as a matter of fact, he would very much sooner have had honey.

When they reached England, the sailor sold the parrot who liked honey to an old lady who lived in a cottage on a hill. She didn't know much about parrots. She didn't know the parrot was a Lory. She didn't know he had a special tongue for licking honey out of flowers. She didn't even know he liked honey.

But she thought his red and green feathers, his gold and blue feathers, and the dark purple feathers on the top of his head were beautiful. She called him Polly, and fed him on bits of bread and biscuit.

Whenever he said, as he often did: 'What have you got, what have you got, what have you got for me?' she would give him a bit of bread or biscuit. But, of course, he would very much sooner have had honey.

Now the old lady lived by herself and had to work very hard to make enough money to buy food. Generally she had just bread and margarine for tea, because she couldn't afford to buy honey even for herself, although she liked it.

Then one day when she wasn't in the least expecting it, the old lady's nephew who lived in South Africa sent her a present. It was a wooden box carefully packed with straw. Some of the straw was already poking between the boards, but it was impossible to tell what was inside.

When the postman brought it, he said: 'Looks like a nice surprise, lady. Maybe some jam or some fruit.'

She carried the box carefully into her sitting room and unfastened it. It wasn't jam or fruit. It was six jars of honey all wrapped up in straw. Inside was a note which said:

Dear Auntie,

I have managed to get a very nice job in South Africa, and I am making quite a bit of money. I am sure you are not able to buy all the things you need, so I am sending you six jars of honey. If you like them, I will send some more.

Love from your nephew – Robert

When she had read the letter she was tremendously excited and pleased, because it was so long since anyone had sent her a present and today it wasn't even her birthday. She took out the jars very carefully and put them in a row in the larder. Then she cleared up all the straw and paper and string, and said to herself: 'I'll start the first jar at teatime today.'

When the clock struck half past three, the old lady put the kettle on the gas, and began to cut some bread. It was certainly rather early for tea, but the old lady was so excited about the honey that she couldn't wait any longer. She put the bread and margarine on the table, took a plate and a knife, and a cup and saucer and spoon out of the cupboard, and then she went to the larder.

All this made Polly very excited. He wasn't in his cage, but on a separate perch where he could turn somersaults if he liked. The old lady let him sit here in the afternoons. He could tell it was teatime, and when the old lady went to the larder he expected she would bring out some cake or fruit.

So he shouted at the top of his voice: 'What have you got, what have you got, what have you got for me?' When the old lady brought out neither cake nor fruit, but only a jar of yellow stuff, Polly was rather puzzled. But as soon as he saw her take some on her knife and spread the sticky stuff on her bread, and eat it with such pleasure, he knew it was honey.

And as soon as he knew it was honey, he knew he absolutely must think of some way of getting it for himself.

The old lady never dreamt of giving the Lory honey. She didn't know much about parrots. She didn't know he was called a Lory. She didn't know he had a tongue specially shaped for getting honey out of flowers. She didn't even know he liked honey.

But all the time the old lady was spreading the honey on her first slice of bread and thinking how wonderfully kind her nephew was to send it, and what an unexpected treat it was, the Lory was working out a plan.

Now parrots, as you know, are very clever at remembering words and also at imitating people, and sometimes when they talk they can make their voice sound as if it is coming from a different part of the house altogether, so that you have no idea it is the parrot talking at all.

While the old lady was eating her bread and honey and enjoying it tremendously, she suddenly heard a *Miaow!* It was really the Lory, but she didn't know that.

'There's a kitten outside,' she said. 'Poor thing, I expect it's lost. I'll let it in so that it can get warm by the fire.' And she went to the door and opened it.

Polly just had time to flutter on to the table and take a mouthful of honey with his special tongue and get on his perch again before she came back.

'How very strange,' she said, 'I'm sure I heard a kitten. Yet I've looked in the street, and there isn't a kitten to be seen.'

Polly winked and shouted: 'What have you got, what have you got, what have you got for me?' But the old lady still didn't know he was after the honey.

While the lady was spreading her *second* slice of bread, he thought of another plan. This time he made a noise like the kettle boiling over.

'Goodness!' cried the old lady, jumping up. 'That will put the stove out, unless I hurry.'

And while she rushed out into the kitchen, Polly flew down and took his second big mouthful of honey.

'That's very peculiar,' said the old lady, coming back again just as Polly scrambled on to his perch. 'The kettle's perfectly all right, and not boiling over at all.' But she still didn't understand the Lory was after her honey.

Then he had what he thought was his best plan of all. He made a noise like big drops of rain falling on the roof.

'Oh heavens!' said the poor old lady. 'Now I shall have to bring all the washing in.'

And she left her tea with the pot of honey standing on the table, and went outside to fetch in the washing before it got soaked.

She was a long time, because she had washed a tablecloth, two sheets, a pillowslip, a towel, a frock, a cardigan and the curtains from the sitting room. And while she was taking them all off the line, the Lory was swallowing honey as fast as he could.

At last, her arms full of washing, the old lady came back into the room. 'That's funny,' she said, as she looked at the window. 'The sun is shining as brightly as ever. I do believe I've brought all the washing in for nothing.'

'And that's funnier still!' she went on with a little scream, looking at the table. 'I do believe someone's been eating my honey!'

She picked up the jar and looked at it. There was just a scraping left at the bottom. Yet she had only opened the jar a few minutes ago.

'It must be a burglar,' she said, and feeling very brave she began to look under the furniture and inside the cupboards and wherever a burglar might find space to hide.

All the time she was hunting, the Lory was turning somersaults on his perch and shrieking at the top of his voice: 'What have you got, what have you got, what have you got for me?' He felt very pleased with himself, and he didn't care a bit that he had made the

old lady go to all the trouble of bringing in her washing, and on top of that had eaten almost the whole of a jar of honey that her nephew had sent from South Africa.

When the old lady had decided there was no burglar in the house, she went back to the tea table. And then she noticed drips of honey leading over the tablecloth, over the floor, and up to Polly's perch. She reached up and touched his perch, and, sure enough, that was sticky too.

'Why, you rascal!' she said. 'I do believe it was you who stole the honey.'

And that was how the old lady who didn't know much about parrots discovered that Lories like honey better than anything else in the world. After that, she always gave her Lory some honey for his tea, and she managed it quite well because her nephew in South Africa sent her six jars every month.

But do you know, she never found out it was the Lory who played those tricks on her just to get a taste of her honey!

How Fire Came to Earth

Grace Hallworth
Illustrated by Rachael Saunders

At the beginning of time, long before man was formed, there was no fire on Earth. Everywhere was cold and bleak and a grey mist shrouded land and sea. Woolly coated creatures huddled together in caves and feathered ones clustered wherever they could find shelter. Some creatures made their homes in the ground, while a few burrowed to the very depths of the earth and were never seen again.

High above Earth the great Sunbird basked in the glow of a fire that burned day and night. He did not know of the suffering of Earth creatures. His home was too far away. At last the creatures could bear the cold no longer so they held a meeting.

When all were gathered Leopard began: 'Two of my litter are dead from cold.'

At this point Seagull interrupted: 'It is hard to find enough shelter to keep our nests warm.'

Every living creature complained about the cold. Only Owl kept silent.

When all had spoken she said: 'Mighty

Thunderbird shoots fire sticks across the sky when he is angry. Let us ask him for some of his fire.'

They chose Eagle to seek him out for he could fly higher than any other creature. Besides, Eagle knew where to find him. He flew to a mountain in the middle of the ocean where Thunderbird rested after his noisy outbursts. There he waited for many days. When Thunderbird arrived, Eagle approached him and said: 'Great one who makes thunder-fire, I come from Earth where many creatures die from cold. Will you give some of your fire to warm Earth?'

'My fire is for the sky,' replied Thunderbird. 'You could not use it on Earth, but my brother has a fire tree. I will ask him to give you a branch from it.'

And he went at once to Sunbird and said: 'Brother, the wretched creatures on Earth perish because of cold. Give them fire so that they may live!'

But Sunbird said: 'No, I will not give them fire. Their knowledge is not sufficient to guard it and they will destroy Earth.'

Again and again Thunderbird pleaded for the Earth creatures but Sunbird would not yield.

One night when his brother was asleep, Thunderbird stole a branch from the fire tree. He fitted it to his bow and shot it down on to the mountain where he had met Eagle. It went straight to the heart of a dead sycamore tree and set it alight. Earth creatures saw the blazing mountain and were anxious to get hold of fire, but Eagle was away and no one knew when he would return. One of them would have to cross the water to get to the blazing mountain before fire died away.

'Whooooo? W-hoohoo-hooo? Whoo will fly to get fire?' called Owl.

'I will. I will. I will fly to the mountain and bring back fire,' said a bird with beautiful silver-grey feathers. And off she flew across the sea. She had never flown so far or so high. She was buffeted by strong winds but held her course and flew steadily on.

On the mountain red-hot flames leapt and crackled and the bird could find no place to alight. She would have to seize a fire stick and return at once. Round and round she flew looking for an opening but as she drew near fire, a change came over her. She felt a tingling, prickling sensation. Grey-black wisps curled and twisted around her eyes and snaked into her mouth. She tried to escape by flying high above them and the cool clean air cleared her eyes and helped her to breathe.

In her breast, the bird felt that she must soon leave, for the struggle with fire had tired her. Cautiously she dropped to a lower air stream just above the fire, where the wisps were small and weak. Once more sharp pains shot through her body and as the stabbing pains increased, her feathers began to fall off. 'Haaargh! Haaargh! Haaargh!' Her harsh cries of pain and fear came from a throat sore from heat and smoke. Her wings were badly burned and the skin on her feet hung like strips of yellow ribbon. She mustered all her strength and lifted herself up and away. She was fortunate that the wind was blowing in the direction of the Homeland. She flew low, and the spray from the waves soothed her aching body.

At the water's edge, the creatures were waiting for the bird to return with fire. Instead, they saw a bedraggled creature with eyes as red as fire itself. Her silvery feathers were blackened. And they have remained that way to this day, for she had become the bird we now call the Raven.

'Whuu did this to you?' howled Wolf.

'It was fire himself. He stabs you with sharp points while his wisps force your eyes shut and squeeze breath from your body. We cannot tame fire,' said the bird.

'I can. No one is swifter than I. I will, I will,

112

I will go to the mountain and seize fire,'
boasted Leopard. Immediately he dived into
the sea and started to swim across the wide
expanse of cold water. Waves as tall as
Leopard tossed him about. Swift treacherous
currents tried to pull him under but his strokes
were powerful.

On the mountain the fire blazed.

Leopard decided to swim around and see
where he could best attack fire. He found a
winding path that led to the top of the
mountain. Suddenly he was enveloped in a
thick black cloud which began to smother
him. His eyes hurt so much that he couldn't
see. Frantically he spun round and round,
trying to escape, but fire was choking the
breath from his body. He was beginning to
weaken when he saw a golden light, and he

rushed through it. It had a sting fiercer than bees robbed of their honey.

He roared a fearful roar, leapt into the air and fell headlong into the sea. It was the cold water that saved him, cooling his feet, his body, his face.

Leopard hurt badly all over. His fur was singed and his legs were stiff. Partly floating and partly swimming, he made his way back home. The creatures were so sure that Leopard would bring fire that they had prepared a large pit in the forest which they filled with leaves and dried seaweed.

'We will tame fire and keep him alive here. Then every creature may take some of fire whenever there is need,' said Owl.

As they waited at the water's edge for

Leopard, they talked of all the things they would do when they had fire.

But what was this?

Could this be graceful Leopard, so fleet of foot?

The creatures could not believe their eyes. Leopard's beautiful golden coat was now threadbare and spotted with black soot. They watched in amazement as he limped away into the forest.

Night, the black curtain, fell, and still fire blazed.

From a distance the Earth creatures watched, glad at least for the warmth that came from fire's brightness.

Who dared to fetch fire now that powerful Leopard had failed?

'WhoooOOO? W-hoo-hoo-hoooo? Whoooooooo?' Owl's mournful cries echoed through the night.

'Let me! Let me! Let me fly to the mountain,' pleaded Bat.

She had been asleep for most of the day. Now she was wide awake.

No one heard Bat's gentle twittering. No one saw the small black creature fly off in the dark. She had no fear of the journey for she was used to travelling long distances, and the thought of bringing back fire spurred her on. As she approached the mountain, she saw fires flare up like rockets, showering sparks everywhere. Bat was spellbound by the bright colours. She flew close, yet felt no pain from fire's light. She darted down to seize a twig of fire and it spat a bunch of sparks right in her eyes. Shrieking, she rose in the air, flying blind, for her eyes were badly burned.

'Can't see! Can't see! Can't see!' she cried.

'Seeseeseek! Seeseeseek! Seeseeseek!' keened the other bats who heard her cry of distress. Their high-pitched calls helped her to find the way back to the Homeland and the creatures who anxiously waited at the water's edge. All gathered around to see what fire had done to Bat.

'Fire paints bright pictures but when you try to take them he throws dust in your eyes. Fire is cruel,' sobbed Bat.

And ever since that night Bat has been blind. She shuns the light of day and lives in dark places.

Snake scolded. 'Iss s-s-so small a creature that s-s-sets out to s-s-steal fire! There musst be no more of thisss foolissness. I will s-s-seek fire if Eagle isss not back s-s-soon.'

Now Spider was going to tell the other creatures about her idea to catch fire and bring him back. But when she heard Snake scolding Bat she said nothing. Instead she crawled away to work on her plan. She would build a bridge across the sea to the mountain and fetch fire. She began to weave a pattern which she had practised so often that she could do the movement in her sleep. As she spun, she sang a song:

'In and out and in and out
Up and down and round about
In and out and in and out
Pay the silken thread far out.'

Again and again she repeated the movements as she sang. Hour after hour she spun her strong silken thread and paid it out. At last her feet touched ground. She had arrived.

Spider scurried around, looking for something to catch fire. It must be:

something flat that would sit on her back
something that would not let water in
something that would not let fire out.

Near the water she found a flat stone, but it could not hold fire in.

Further along the beach she saw a piece of wood. Fire had burned a hole through it.

Dawn flooded the sky, reflecting the colours of fire below.

Spider searched everywhere.

Half-buried in the sand she saw a shell. It was flat enough to sit on her back and hollow enough to keep fire in and water out. Spider carried it to where fire was burning brightest.

Phtt! Phtt! A small piece of burning wood broke off from a branch and flew into the shell. At once Spider placed the shell on her back and set out for the bridge she had woven. When she got there fire had destroyed the silken bridge.

She didn't know what to do. Fire was spreading and soon there would be no place to stand. There was no other way out. She would have to go into the sea.

But Spider couldn't swim!

Then she remembered that whenever she saw the tide coming in at dawn, it flowed

gently into shore. Could she risk going into the sea with fire on her back? She would have to hurry, for already she could see a faint glow of morning light through the night curtain. Quickly she spun a sticky bell-shaped web under her body to keep her afloat. She stepped bravely into the sea.

All morning Spider floated on the gentle tide stream towards Homeland. She was sleepy and tired but dared not sleep for she didn't know when the tide might become choppy and fast. She sang a song to keep herself awake:

'Rock and sway and rock and sway
Tide stream flow in all the way
Rock and sway and rock and sway
Fire safe from briny spray.'

At last the tide washed her up on the shore where she had left the others. All the creatures had gone home! There was no one to greet Spider or to lift the shell off her back. She struggled up the beach and along the path to the pit in the forest. But now, fire was beginning to burn through the shell and Spider could feel the heat on her back and the hairs of her legs. At last she could bear the pain no more. She tilted fire on the ground and curled up in a tight ball to protect herself. Greedily, fire licked the ground round the frightened creature, ready to devour her. And he would have done so – but Eagle returned just then and saw what was happening. He swooped down, and gripped Spider in his talons and took her away to safety near the forest pool.

And so it was that this tiny creature

conquered fire and brought it to the Homeland so that all the Earth's creatures might have warmth. Spider knows that fire lurks in the forest waiting for a chance to punish her, so she lives in water where fire cannot reach her. The water spider still carries the splash of colour where fire marked her.

Theseus and the Minotaur

Retold by Charles Kingsley
Illustrated by Ruthine Burton

Long ago there ruled a great king in Athens called Aegeus, and his son, Theseus, was a hero who had done many brave and mighty deeds.

Now the whole country was happy and at peace except for one great sorrow. Minos,

King of Crete, had fought against the Athenians and had conquered them; and before returning to Crete he had made a hard and cruel peace. Each year the Athenians were forced to send seven young men and seven maidens to be sacrificed to the Minotaur. This was a monster who lived in the labyrinth, a winding path among rocks and caves. So each spring seven youths and maidens, chosen by lot, journeyed in a ship with black sails to the shores of Crete, to be torn to pieces by the savage Minotaur.

One spring, when the herald from King Minos arrived, Theseus determined to make an end of the beast, and rid his father's people of this horrible evil. He went and told Aegeus that when the black-sailed ship set out on the morrow he would go too and slay the Minotaur.

'But how will you slay him, my son?' said Aegeus. 'For you must leave your club and your shield behind, and be cast to the monster, defenceless and naked like the rest.'

And Theseus said, 'Are there no stones in that labyrinth; and have I not fists and teeth?'

Then Aegeus clung to his knees; but he would not hear; and at last he let him go, weeping bitterly, and said only these words –

'Promise me but this, if you return in peace, though that may hardly be: take down the black sail of the ship (for I shall watch for it all day upon the cliffs), and hoist instead a white sail, that I may know from far off that you are safe.'

And Theseus promised, and went out to the marketplace where the herald stood, while they drew lots for the youths and maidens who were to sail in that doleful crew. And the people stood wailing and weeping as the lot fell on this one and on that; but Theseus strode into the midst, and cried,

'Here is a youth who needs no lot. I myself will be one of the seven.'

And the herald asked in wonder, 'Fair youth, know you whither you are going?'

And Theseus said, 'I know. Let us go down to the black-sailed ship.'

So they went down to the black-sailed ship, seven maidens, and seven youths, and Theseus before them all, and the people following them, lamenting. But Theseus whispered to his companions, 'Have hope, for the monster is not immortal.' Then their hearts were comforted a little; but they wept as they went on board, and the cliffs of Sunium, and all the isles of the Aegean Sea, rang with the voice of their lamentations as they sailed on towards their deaths in Crete.

And at last they came to Crete, and to Knossos, beneath the peaks of Ida, and to the palace of Minos the great king, to whom Zeus himself taught laws – so he was the wisest of all mortal kings, and conquered all the Aegean isles; and his ships were as many as the seagulls, and his palace was like a marble hill.

But Theseus stood before Minos, and they looked each other in the face. And Minos bade take them to prison, and cast them to the monster one by one. Then Theseus cried,

'A boon, O Minos! Let me be thrown first to the beast. For I came hither for that very purpose, of my own will, and not by lot.'

'Who art thou, then, brave youth?'

'I am the son of him whom of all men thou hatest most, Aegeus, the King of Athens, and I have come here to end this matter.'

And Minos pondered awhile, looking steadfastly at him, and he answered at last mildly,

'Go back in peace, my son. It is a pity that one so brave should die.'

But Theseus said, 'I have sworn that I will not go back till I have seen the monster face to face.'

And at that Minos frowned, and said, 'Then thou shalt see him; take the madman away.'

And they led Theseus away into prison, with the other youths and maidens.

But Ariadne, Minos's daughter, saw him, as she came out of her white stone hall; and she loved him for his courage and his majesty, and said, 'Shame that such a youth should die!' And by night she went down to the prison, and told him all her heart, and said,

'Flee down to your ship at once, for I have bribed the guards before the door. Flee, you and all your friends, and go back in peace to Greece; and take me, take me with you! for I dare not stay after you are gone; for my father will kill me miserably, if he knows what I have done.'

And Theseus stood silent a while; for he was astonished and confounded by her beauty. But at last he said, 'I cannot go home in peace, till I have seen and slain this Minotaur, and avenged the deaths of the youths and maidens, and put an end to the terrors of my land.'

'And will you kill the Minotaur? How, then?'

'I know not, nor do I care. But he must be strong if he be too strong for me.'

Then she loved him all the more, and said, 'But when you have killed him, how will you find your way out of the labyrinth?'

'I know not, neither do I care. But it must be a strange road, if I do not find it out before I have eaten up the monster's carcass.'

Then she loved him all the more, and said,

'Fair youth, you are too bold; but I can help you, weak as I am. I will give you a sword, and with that perhaps you may slay the beast; and a clue of thread, and by that, perhaps, you may find your way out again. Only promise me that if you escape safely you will take me home with you to Greece; for my father will surely kill me, if he knows what I have done.'

Then Theseus laughed and said, 'Am I not safe enough now?' And he hid the sword in his bosom, and rolled up the clue in his hand; and then he swore to Ariadne, and fell down before her and kissed her hands and her feet; and she wept over him a long while, and then went away; and Theseus lay down and slept sweetly. When the evening came, the guards arrived and led him away to the labyrinth.

And he went down into that doleful gulf, through winding paths among the rocks, under caverns, and arches, and galleries, and over heaps of fallen stone. And he turned on the left hand, and on the right hand, and went up and down, till his head was dizzy; but all the while he held his clue. For when he went in he had fastened it to a stone, and left it to unroll out of his hand as he went on; and it lasted him till he met the Minotaur, in a narrow chasm between black cliffs.

And when he saw him he stopped a while, for he had never seen so strange a beast. His body was a man's; but his head was the head of a bull, and his teeth were the teeth of a lion, and with them he tore his prey. And when he saw Theseus, he roared, and put his head down, and rushed right at him.

But Theseus stepped aside nimbly, and as he passed by, cut him in the knee; and ere he could turn in the narrow path, he followed him, and stabbed him again and again from behind, till the monster fled bellowing wildly; for he never before had felt a wound. And Theseus followed him at full speed, holding the clue of thread in his left hand.

Then on, through cavern after cavern, under

dark ribs of sounding stone, and up rough glens and torrent-beds, among the sunless roots of Ida, and to the edge of the eternal snow, went they, the hunter and the hunted, while the hills bellowed to the monster's bellow.

And at last Theseus came up with him, where he lay panting on a slab among the snows, and caught him by the horns, and forced his head back, and drove the keen sword through his throat.

Then he turned, and went back limping and weary, feeling his way down by the clue of thread, till he came to the mouth of that doleful place; and saw waiting for him, whom but Ariadne!

And he whispered, 'It is done!' and showed her the sword; and she laid her finger on her lips and led him to the prison, and opened the doors, and set all the prisoners free, while the guards lay sleeping heavily; for she had silenced them with wine.

Then they fled to their ship together, and leapt on board, and hoisted up the sail; and the night lay dark around them, so that they passed through Minos's ships, and escaped all safe to Naxos; and there Ariadne became Theseus's wife.

But that fair Ariadne never came to Athens with her husband. Some say that Theseus left her sleeping on Naxos among the Cyclades; and that Dionysus the wine king found her, and took her up into the sky. And some say that Dionysus drove away Theseus, and took Ariadne from him by force; but however that may be, in his haste or in his grief, Theseus forgot to put up the white sail. Now Aegeus his father sat and watched on Sunium, day after day, and strained his old eyes across the sea to see the ship from afar. And when he saw the black sail, and not the white one, he gave up Theseus for dead, and in his grief he fell into the sea, and died; so it is called the Aegean to this day.

And now Theseus was King of Athens, and he guarded it and ruled it well.

Patrick Comes to School

Margaret Mahy
Illustrated by Rachael Saunders

'Graham,' said the teacher, 'will you look after Patrick at playtime? Remember he is new to the school and has no friends here yet.'

There were lots of things Graham would

rather have done, but he had to smile and say, 'Yes, Mr Porter.'

Behind him Harry Biggs gave his funny, grunting laugh and whispered, 'Nursey-nursey Graham.' Mr Porter was watching, so Graham could not say anything back.

Patrick was a little shrimp of a boy with red hair – not just carroty or ginger – a sort of fiery red. Freckles were all over his face, crowded like people on a five o'clock bus, all jostling and pushing to get the best places. In fact, Graham thought, Patrick probably had more freckles than face. As well as red hair and freckles, Patrick had a tilted nose and eyes so blue and bright that he looked all the time as if he'd just been given a specially good Christmas present. He seemed cheerful, which was something, but he was a skinny, short little fellow, not likely to be much good at sport, or at looking after himself in a fight.

Just my luck to get stuck with a new boy! thought Graham.

At playtime he took Patrick round and showed him the football field and the shelter shed. Graham's friend, Len, came along too. Len and Graham were very polite to Patrick, and he was very polite back, but it wasn't much fun really. Every now and then Len and Graham would look at each other over Patrick's head. It was easy to do, because he was so small. 'Gosh, what a nuisance!' the looks said, meaning Patrick.

Just before the bell went, Harry Biggs came up with three other boys. Harry Biggs *was* big, and the three other boys were even bigger, and came from another class.

'Hello, here's the new boy out with his nurse,' said Harry. 'What's your name, new boy?'

Graham felt he ought to do something to protect little Patrick, but Patrick spoke out quite boldly and said, 'Patrick Fingall O'Donnell.' So that was all right.

Harry Biggs frowned at the name. 'Now don't be too smart!' he said. 'We tear cheeky little kids apart in this school, don't we?' He nudged the other boys, who grinned and shuffled. 'Where do you live, O'Donnell?'

Then Patrick said a funny thing. 'I live in a house among the trees, and we've got a golden bird sitting on our gate.'

He didn't sound as if he was joking. He spoke carefully as if he was asking Harry Biggs a difficult riddle. He sounded as if, in a minute, he might be laughing at Harry Biggs. Harry Biggs must have thought so too, because he frowned even harder and said, 'Remember what I told you, and don't be too clever. Now listen . . . what does your father do?'

'Cut it out, Harry,' said Graham quickly. 'Pick on someone your own size.'

'I'm not hurting him, Nursey!' exclaimed Harry. 'Go on, Ginger, what does he do for a crust?'

Patrick answered quickly, almost as if he was reciting a poem.

'My father wears clothes with gold all over them,' said Patrick. 'In the morning he says to the men 'I'll have a look at my elephants this morning,' and he goes and looks at his elephants. When he says the word, the elephants kneel down. He can ride the elephants all day if he wants to, but mostly he is too busy with the lions or his monkeys or his bears.'

Harry Biggs stared at Patrick with his eyes popping out of his head.

'Who do you think you're kidding?' he said at last. 'Are you making out your dad's a king or something? Nobody wears clothes with gold on them.'

'My father does!' said Patrick. 'Wears them every day!' He thought for a moment. 'All these lions and tigers lick his hands,' he added.

'Does he work in a circus?' asked one of the other boys.

'No!' said Patrick. 'We'd live in a caravan then, not a house with a golden bird at the gate.' Once again Graham felt that Patrick was turning his answers into riddles.

Before anyone could say any more, the bell rang for them to go back into school.

'Gee, you'll hear all about that!' Len said to Patrick. 'Why did you tell him all that stuff?'

'It's true,' Patrick said. 'He asked me, and it's true.'

'He'll think you were taking the mickey,' Graham said. 'Anyway, it couldn't be true.'

'It *is* true,' said Patrick, 'and it isn't taking the mickey to say what's true, is it?'

'Well, I don't know,' Graham muttered to Len. 'It doesn't sound very true to me.'

Of course Harry Biggs and the other boys spread the story round the school.

Children came up to Patrick and said, 'Hey, does your father wear pure gold?'

'Not all gold,' said Patrick. 'Just quite a lot.'

Then the children would laugh and pretend to faint with laughing.

'Hey, Ginger!' called Harry Biggs. 'How's all the elephants?'

'All right, thank you,' Patrick would reply politely. Once he added, 'We've got a monkey too, at present, and he looks just like you.' But he only said it once, because Harry Biggs pulled his hair and twisted his ears. Patrick's ears were nearly as red as his hair.

'Serves you right for showing off,' said Graham.

'Well, I might have been showing off a bit,' Patrick admitted. 'It's hard not to sometimes.'

Yet, although they teased him, slowly

children came to like Patrick. Graham liked him a lot. He was so good-tempered and full of jokes. Even when someone was laughing at him, he laughed too. The only thing that worried Graham was the feeling that Patrick was laughing at some secret joke, or at any rate at some quite different thing.

'Don't you get sick of being teased?' he asked.

'Well, I'm a bit sick of it now,' Patrick said, 'but mostly I don't mind. Anyhow, what I said was true, and that's all there is to say.'

'I'd hate to be teased so much,' Graham said. But he could see Patrick was like a rubber ball – the harder you knocked him down, the faster and higher he bounced back.

The wonderful day came when the class

was taken to the zoo. Even Harry Biggs, who usually made fun of school outings, looked forward to this one.

Off they went in the school bus, and Mr Porter took them round.

'. . . Like the Pied Piper of Hamelin,' said Patrick, 'with all the rats following him.'

'Who are you calling a rat, Ginger?' said Harry Biggs sourly.

Everywhere at the zoo was the smell of animals, birds and straw. They had a map which showed them the quickest way to go round the zoo, and the first lot of cages they went past held birds. There were all sizes and colours of birds from vultures to canaries. One cage held several bright parrots. The parrots watched the children pass with round, wise eyes. Then suddenly the biggest of the

lot flew from his perch and clung to the wire peering out at them.

'Patrick! Hallo, Patrick dear!' it said. 'Hallo! Hallo! Hallo, Patrick! Hallo, dear!'

Mr Porter looked at Patrick.

'Oh yes,' he said. 'I forgot about you, Patrick. It's a bit of a busman's holiday for you, isn't it?'

As they walked away the parrot went on screaming after them, 'Hallo, Patrick! Patrick! Hallo, dear!' in its funny, parrot voice.

On they went past the lions and tigers. Len and Graham stole sideways glances at Patrick, and so did Harry Biggs and several other children. Patrick looked as wide-eyed and interested as anyone else. He did not seem to see the glances at all.

They went past the bear pits, and then up a hill where there was nothing but trees. Among the trees, beside a stone fence, was a little house. On one of the gateposts was a brass peacock, polished until it shone, and below that was a little notice saying 'Head Keeper's Cottage'.

Now, for the first time, Patrick suddenly turned and grinned at Graham.

'*That*'s where I live,' he whispered.

They were all looking into the bear pits ten minutes later when a man came hurrying to meet them. He was wearing a lot of gold braid all over his blue uniform. There was gold braid round his cap and his brass buttons shone like little suns. His eyes were blue and bright and his face was covered with freckles – more freckle than face you might have said. He stopped to speak to Mr Porter and took off his cap.

His hair was as red as fire.

'Is *that* your father?' Graham asked.

'Yes,' said Patrick. 'See, I told you he wore a lot of gold.'

'Huh!' said Harry Biggs. 'Well, why didn't you say when I asked you . . . why didn't you say he was a keeper at the zoo?'

'Head Keeper!' said Graham, feeling suddenly very proud of Patrick.

'Ordinary keepers don't have gold,' Patrick pointed out.

'Why didn't you say?' Harry repeated. 'Trying to be clever, eh?'

'I don't like things to sound too ordinary,' said Patrick, sounding rather self-satisfied. 'I like them to be noble and sort of mysterious.'

'Well, you're mad,' said Harry, but no one was taking any notice of him. Mr Porter and Mr O'Donnell, Head Keeper, came back to them.

'This is Mr O'Donnell,' said Mr Porter. 'He has offered to let us have a look at the young lion cubs. They aren't on view to the public yet, so we are very lucky. And don't worry – the mother lion won't be there, so none of you will get eaten.'

As they went on their way a foolish little girl said to Patrick, 'Have you got any other relatives who do interesting things, Patrick?'

'Shut up!' said Graham, but it was too late.

'My uncle,' said Patrick, without any hesitation. 'He's my great-uncle really, though. He eats razor blades for a living, razor blades and burning matches.'

'No one can eat razor blades!' shouted Harry Biggs.

'Well, my great-uncle does,' said Patrick and this time everyone believed him.

PS. Patrick's great-uncle was a magician.

The Rajah's Ears

Michael Rosen
Illustrated by Ruthine Burton

Once, long ago in India when there were kings called rajahs and people lived in fear of them, there was a rajah who had very big ears. They were so big he wore a special hat to hide them. All day and every day he wore his hat so that no one would know about his ears. Of course, one or two people did know about them, but they didn't say a word to anyone else about it. They could imagine what terrible things would happen to them if the rajah ever found out that they had been gossiping about him.

The rajah was going to get married and so he wanted to have his hair cut.

He ordered a barber to come to the palace, and when he arrived he sent all his servants and courtiers outside.

Then he said to the barber,

'Now listen here, young man, in a moment I am going to take my hat off. Then you will see that I have ears that are not small. No one in the whole country knows about my ears. If ever I hear that you have been talking about my ears, gossiping or telling tales, then I shall cut your head off. If I ever hear that anyone knows about my ears, I will know that you told them, and I will do as I say, I will cut your head off. Do you understand?'

'Yes, your majesty,' said the barber.

The rajah took his hat off and the barber cut his hair. All the time he was cutting away with his scissors, he was trying not to look at the rajah's ears. But they were right in front of him all the time, just where he was looking.

So he said over and over again to himself,

'I must not tell anyone about the rajah's ears, I must not tell anyone about the rajah's ears.'

When he had finished, the rajah put his hat on and sent the barber off saying, 'Remember what I said, young man.'

'Yes, your majesty, not a word to anyone.'

And that's the way it was, for the rest of the day; he didn't breathe a word about it to anyone at all. But all the time, the barber was thinking about it. At work, the next day, when he was cutting other people's hair, and chatting with a customer, he was thinking about it. The customer says, 'I don't suppose much happens to you here, does it? Day in, day out, cutting people's hair?'

Straightaway, the thought of the rajah's big ears leapt into his mind. 'Well, sir,' he says, 'the other day I was cutting the rajah's hair and you won't believe it but you know he's got enormous—'

And he stopped himself. *What am I saying?* he thought, *I'll get my head cut off.*

'What's he got?' said the customer.

'Enormous jewels on his rings,' said the barber.

Phew, that was a close one, he said to himself.

At home that night, his wife was changing her earrings and he found himself saying, 'Those earrings look very nice on you, my dear.'

'Thank you,' says his wife, 'you don't think they're too small?'

'They don't look too small on you dear, but I tell you who they *would* look funny on – that's the rajah because he's got really big ear—'

What am I saying? he said to himself. *I'll get my head cut off.*

'What's he got?' said the wife.

'He's got really big earrings. Small ones would look funny on him.'

Phew, that was another close one, he thought.

Outside in the yard, his children were playing and he went out to call them in for bedtime.

Two of them were pulling faces at each other, sticking their tongues out and pulling their ears.

'Don't do that,' says the barber, 'you look like the rajah.'

'Why do we look like the rajah?' says one.

'Because he's got big—'

What am I saying? the barber thought, *I'll get my head cut off.*

'He's got big children,' said the barber, 'and they look like the rajah. You look like his children . . . so you look like the rajah.'

Phew, that was another close one.

And so it went on all the next day. He was dying to tell someone. In the end he had a plan. The next morning, instead of going straight to work, he went off to the woods.

I know what I'll do, he thought, *I'll tell a tree. I'll tell a tree that the rajah's got big ears and that'll be that. It won't bother me any more. I'll have told someone who can't tell anyone else. The rajah will never find out, and I'll feel a lot better.*

So the barber crept up to a great big tree in the woods. He looked behind him and to either side. He looked behind the tree and all around it and then he stood up in front of it and said,

'The rajah's got big ears.'

Oooh, that felt so much better. It felt like

a great load had been taken off his back and off he went to work happier than he had been for days.

Later that day, a woodcutter came to the woods and chopped down the very same tree that the barber had talked to. The woodcutter sold the wood from the tree to a musical instrument maker and the instrument maker made some drums called tabla and a stringed instrument called a sitar.

The instrument maker sold the tabla and sitar to a band that was one of the best in the country. In fact, so good was this band, that they were asked to play at the rajah's wedding.

Everyone was there, all the rajah's relations, all his servants, all his servants' servants, even the rajah's barber.

What a day it was. There was a wonderful

ceremony, followed by a great feast and then came the dance.

The musicians made ready, there was a hush and then the music began.

But of all surprising and awful things to happen, the sound coming out of the musical instruments wasn't a wedding dance but a song, and the words of the song were:

'The rajah's got big ears,
oh yes, the rajah's got big ears,
do you know what,
I know what,
the rajah's got big ears.'

'Stop, stop, stop,' shouted the rajah.

'I heard that,' he roared, 'I heard every word of that.'

The hundreds of wedding guests stood in silence.

The thought of his barber sprang into the rajah's mind. Only the barber knew about his ears, only the barber could have told anyone.

'BARBER!' bellowed the rajah, 'barber, where are you?'

The barber stepped forward.

'Yes, your majesty?'

'I heard that song. You heard that song. You have disobeyed me. I told you not to tell a single person and now everyone knows.'

'But your majesty, I didn't tell a single person.'

'Oh yes, you did, and tonight you lose your head.'

'But, your majesty, I didn't tell a single

person. I told a tree. That's not a person, is it?'

The rajah stopped. A smile crept on to his face.

He muttered to himself.

'I didn't tell a person. "I told a tree." The man's right, he didn't tell a single person. Oh, what am I making a fuss about? It's only ears. So what if I have got big ears? Some people have got big feet, some people have got little noses. We're all different and we always will be.'

At that, he pulled off his hat and said,

'Friends and relations, the rajah's got big ears. Let the band play.'

The band played and everyone sang.

'The rajah's got big ears,

oh yes, the rajah's got big ears,

do you know what,

I know what,

the rajah's got big ears.'

Strange Animal

Alexander McCall Smith
Illustrated by Rachael Saunders

There were many people to tell that boy what to do. There was his mother and his father, his grandfather, and his older brother. And there was also an aunt, who was always saying 'Do this. Do that.' Every day this aunt would shout at him, and make a great noise that would frighten the birds.

The boy did not like his aunt. Sometimes he thought that he might go to some man to buy some medicine to put into her food to make her quiet, but of course he never did this. In spite of all his aunt's shouting and ordering about, the boy always obeyed her, as his father said he must.

'She has nothing to do but shout at you,' the boy's father explained. 'It keeps her happy.'

'When I'm a big man I'll come and shout in her ear,' the boy said. It was good to think about that.

There was a place that the aunt knew where a lot of fruit grew. It was a place which was quite far away, and the boy did not like going there. Near this place there were caves, and the boy had heard that a strange animal lived in these caves. One of his friends had seen this strange animal and had warned people about going near that place.

But the aunt insisted on sending the boy to pick fruit there, and so he went, his heart a cold stone of fear inside him. He found the trees and began to pick the fruit, but a little later he heard the sound of something in the bush beside him. He stopped his task and stood near the tree in case the strange animal should be coming.

Out of the bush came the strange animal. It was just as his friend had described it and the boy was very frightened. Quickly he took out the drum which he had brought with him and began to beat it. The strange animal stopped, looked at the boy in surprise, and began to dance.

All day the boy played the drum, keeping the strange animal dancing. As long as he played the drum, he knew that there was nothing that the strange animal could do to harm him. At last, when night came, the strange animal stopped dancing and disappeared back into the bush. The boy knew that it had gone back to its cave and so he was able to walk home safely. When he reached home, though, his aunt had prepared her shouting.

'Where is all the fruit?' she shouted. Thinking that he had eaten it, she then began to beat him until the boy was able to run away from her and hide in his own hut.

The boy told his father the next day of the

real reason why he had been unable to bring back fruit from the tree. He explained that there had been a strange animal there and that he had had to play his drum to keep the animal dancing. The father listened and told the story to the aunt, who scoffed at the boy.

'There are no strange animals at that place,' she said. 'You must be making all this up.'

But the father believed the boy and said that the next day they would all go to the fruit place with him. The aunt thought that this was a waste of time, but she was not going to miss any chance of shouting, and so she came too.

When all the family reached the tree there was no strange animal. The aunt began to pick fruit from the tree and stuff it into her mouth. Calling to the boy to give her his drum, she hung it on the branch of a tree in a place where he would not be able to get at it easily.

'You must pick fruit,' she shouted to the boy. 'You must not play a drum in idleness.'

The boy obeyed his aunt, but all the time he was listening for any sounds to come from the bush. He knew that sooner or later the strange animal would appear and that they would then all be in danger.

When the strange animal did come, it went straight to the boy's father and mother and quickly ate them up. Then the aunt tried to run away, but the strange animal ran after her and ate her too. While this was happening, the boy had time to reach up for his drum from the branch of the fruit tree. Quickly he began to play this drum, which made the

strange animal stop looking for people to eat and begin to dance.

As the boy played his drum faster and faster, the strange animal danced more and more quickly. Eventually the boy played so fast that the animal had to spit out the father and the mother. The boy was very pleased with this and began to play more slowly. At this, the strange animal's dancing became slower.

'You must play your drum fast again,' the boy's father said. 'Then the strange animal will have to spit out your aunt.'

'Do I have to?' the boy asked, disappointed that he would not be allowed to leave the aunt in the stomach of the strange animal.

'Yes,' the boy's father said sternly. 'You must.'

Reluctantly, the boy again began to play the

drum and the strange animal began to dance more quickly. After a few minutes it was dancing so quickly that it had to spit out the aunt. Then darkness came and the strange animal went back to its cave.

The aunt was very quiet during the journey back home. The next day she was quiet as well, and she never shouted at the boy again. Being swallowed by a strange animal had taught the aunt not to waste her time shouting; now, all that she wanted to do was to sit quietly in the sun.

The boy was very happy.

Vardiello

Retold by Geoffrey Summerfield
Illustrated by Ruthine Burton

There was once a very sensible woman who lived with her only son. His name was Vardiello, and he was a real fool.

One day, the mother had to run an errand, so she said to her silly lad: 'Now, listen. I've got to go out for an hour or two. The old hen in the shed is sitting on a dozen eggs, and they should be hatching out soon. So you must make sure she stays on the eggs and keeps them warm. If she wanders off to go scratching about in the yard, just look sharp and see that she gets back to the nest, double quick. Or we shall have no chickens. You understand?'

'Don't you worry about a thing. I'll take care of everything.'

'And one more thing. That new pot in the cupboard. If you so much as nibble what's in that pot, you'll be dead before you can say Jack Robinson. So leave well alone.'

'Thanks for the warning. I'll go nowhere near it.'

Now, as soon as his mother had gone, Vardiello went into the garden, and he dug holes all over, and covered them with twigs and clods, to try to catch the lads that used to come scrumping in the apple trees. He worked hard for an hour or more, and he was just rubbing his aching back when he saw the old hen come waddling into the garden for a good scratch around.

'Back you go! Shoo! Shoo! Hish! Hish! Back to your eggs! Go on!'

But the hen just ignored him. So he stamped his feet. Then he threw his cap at her. But it made no difference. The old hen just went on with her scratching. So Vardiello got into a real panic, and he picked up a big stick and threw it at her!

Bonk! It hit the poor old hen right on the head, and there she lay, in the dust, dead as a doornail.

'Oh, the eggs! The chickens!' Vardiello

cried. And he rushed into the shed. He put his hand on the eggs and they were almost stone-cold. So he sat on them, to warm them up again, and his trousers were plastered with smashed eggs. What a mess! He tried to scrape it all off, but his hands were just smeared with goo, so he wriggled out of his trousers and washed them in the kitchen sink. He didn't have time to dry them, and they were his only pair, so he put them on again while they were still sopping wet, and his legs felt clammy from top to bottom.

By this time, he was so hungry that his stomach was rumbling like thunder. So he went out and found the poor old hen. He plucked her and cleaned her, lit a fire in the grate, and cooked her.

When the old hen was well cooked, he put

her just outside the kitchen door to cool off. Then he decided to do himself proud, and spread a clean cloth on the table. Then he went down to the cellar with a large jug to get some wine to drink with his meal: in those days, people didn't drink tea, but used to keep a great barrel of wine in the cellar, to drink with their meals.

So he put his jug under the tap of the barrel, and turned the tap on. He was watching all the bubbles sparkling in the jug, when he heard a terrible clattering and banging upstairs. So he rushed out of the cellar, and there were two great tomcats fighting over his chicken!

He chased those cats all over the yard, and they dashed into the house to hide. So he chased them all over the house, upstairs and downstairs, until the cats dropped the old hen under the bed. By the time he'd picked it up and cleaned it, he suddenly remembered the wine tap: it was still running!

So he dashed down to the cellar, and the barrel was empty. The wine was all over the floor, a great flood. Now he had to work out a plan to prevent his mother from finding out. He took a sack of flour, and scattered it all over the cellar floor, to soak up all the wine.

Then he sat down, and thought. *No fat hen! No eggs! No chickens! No wine! No flour! No hope!*

He didn't dare face his mother when she came back, so he decided to do away with himself. He remembered what she had said about the new pot in the cupboard. She'd said he would die if he even nibbled whatever was in that pot. So he rushed up out of the cellar,

slipping and sliding on the flour paste on the floor, and rushed to the cupboard. He snatched the pot off the shelf and gulped down everything, *glug, glug, munch, munch,* until the pot was empty.

Then he went and hid in the oven, and waited to die.

When his mother got back, she knocked and knocked. She had always told him to lock the door when she went out, so she waited for him to come and open it. She knocked and knocked, then she knocked again until her knuckles were sore. Then she lost her patience and kicked the door open.

'Vardiello! Vardiello! Where are you? What are you up to? Are you deaf? Come out, come out, wherever you are! Do you hear?'

And a thin squeaky voice came out of the oven: 'I'm in here. In the oven. But you'll never see me again. I shall be dead in a minute!'

'Don't talk daft!'

'But I shall. I've eaten the poison in the pot. And I'm dying.'

Then his mother sat down and laughed until she cried. The tears poured down her face, and her handkerchief was soaking wet.

'Tell me all about it,' she said, when she could speak. 'You silly billy! Tell me what happened.'

So he told her all about the old hen, the eggs, the cats, the wine, the flour, and the poison in the pot.

'Oh, the pot!' his mother said. 'It was full of pickled walnuts. I was saving them for a rainy day. I just didn't want you to eat them.

So I warned you to leave well alone! But they weren't poison. You'll just have a stomach ache. Now come out of that oven and stretch your legs.'

So Vardiello clambered out of the oven. And he felt very foolish. Then his mother gave him a glass of milk.

'Now, what are we going to do for food?' she asked him. 'No eggs. No chickens. No hen. No flour. No wine. Dear me, I shall have to sell that cloth I've been weaving.'

So she went up to her bedroom and came down with her arms full of a great roll of fine cloth.

'Take this into the market and sell it,' she told Vardiello. 'But be careful. People who talk a lot, and use big words, are probably trying to cheat you. So be on your guard.'

'Don't you worry about a thing,' Vardiello told his mother, and carried the cloth off to market. 'Cloth! Fine cloth!' he shouted. But whenever anybody said 'I'd like to buy some of your cloth,' he remembered what his mother had said. *They talk too much*, he thought, so he didn't sell even a square inch, for fear of being cheated. 'Cloth! Cloth!' he shouted, over and over again, for hours on end, until he was worn out. Then he wandered off, out of the marketplace, until he came to a statue. His feet were sore by this time, that he sat on the ground to rest, and leaned against the statue.

A customer! he thought, looking at the statue. *He could do with some cloth to make some new clothes.*

'Would you like to buy some cloth?' he asked the statue.

No reply.

'It's very good. Don't you like the look of it?'

No reply.

'This is the man for me,' Vardiello whispered.

'It will suit you, sir,' he said to the statue. 'I'll leave it with you. Then you can have a good look at it. You can pay me tomorrow. I'll come back then.'

Then he rushed home to tell his mother all about his success.

'Oh, you silly boy! You can't be trusted to do anything! What am I going to do with you?'

'But, but, Mother, wait till tomorrow. You'll see. I'll get the money for your cloth. Just wait and see.'

The next day, Vardiello rushed off to collect his money from the statue. He had left the cloth by the feet of the statue and, of course, the first person to pass that way had walked off with it.

'I've come for my money. The money for the cloth I left with you yesterday.'

The statue said nothing.

'My money!' Vardiello shouted. 'Money for the cloth.'

The statue said not a word.

'My money!' Vardiello shouted. He was almost weeping with anger by this time, and he rushed to pick up a brick and hurled it at the statue.

And lo and behold, the statue smashed to smithereens! And inside the broken statue, Vardiello found a pot full of gold coins.

Vardiello snatched it up, and laughed out loud. Then he ran all the way home.

'Mother! Mother! Payment! Money for the cloth!'

When his mother saw the pot full of gold coins she was amazed. Then she thought, *Vardiello is going to tell everybody about this gold. I must do something, quick!*

'Thank you, son. Put it all in the cupboard. Then go to the front door and wait for the milkman. I don't want to miss him.'

So Vardiello went and sat just outside the front door. And his mother went upstairs, opened the bedroom window, and dropped a shower of nuts and raisins, currants, figs and dates on the lad. Vardiello couldn't believe his eyes. He caught them in his hands and in his mouth, then he called out to his mother.

'Mother! Mother! It's raining figs, and

dates, and nuts, and raisins! Bring a bowl! Quick!'

So his mother slipped downstairs very quietly on tiptoe and collected her nuts and dates and the currants and raisins in a bowl. And she let Vardiello eat till he was fit to burst, and fell asleep.

A few weeks later, two men were arguing in the street. One of them had found a gold coin in his back garden, and his neighbour was trying to claim it for his own. Vardiello heard them and said, 'Ridiculous! Arguing about a single gold coin! I found a whole potful of them!'

So the men dragged him off to the police station, and the chief of police said to Vardiello. 'Now, my young man, tell me all about your pot of gold.'

'It's very simple, sir. I found it a few weeks ago inside a dumb man who stole a roll of my mother's cloth, on the day it rained figs, and raisins, and currants, and nuts, and . . .'

'A fine tail our cat's got,' said the chief of police. 'Now, run along, my lad, and don't let your imagination run away with you!'

And Vardiello and his mother lived happily ever after. Whenever they needed food, they took a coin out of the pot in their cupboard, and nobody ever believed a word of Vardiello's story.

The Macaronies
Who Went for a Walk

Miloš Macourek
Translated by Marie Burg
Illustrated by Rachael Saunders

To live in a box and never see a thing –
that must be an awful bore. There they
were, lying in a box in the larder, bored stiff:
about one hundred and twenty sticks of

macaroni. They were Italian macaronies, so they spoke to each other in Italian.

'What a bore,' they said, 'what a bore.'

'It's so boring,' said one macaroni, 'we're bored to the teeth – in fact, we could end up eating one another.'

'Well, we can't eat one another raw,' said macaroni number three. 'But why don't we go somewhere? The world is so interesting, after all. It has merry-go-rounds and swings and all sorts of concerts, fancy restaurants, zoos, and goodness knows what else.'

'All right,' said macaroni number nine, 'but will they let us go? People will see us and they'll say, 'Ah! Macaronies!' and they'll grab hold of us, and that'll be the end of our walk.'

'We mustn't be recognised,' said macaroni number thirty-seven, 'so let's wear hats and raincoats.'

So they put on hats and raincoats and off they went. They walked the streets, all one hundred and twenty of them, and people said, 'Look! Some sort of guided tour.'

From time to time the macaronies stopped people who were passing by and asked in Italian, 'Excuse us, do you know any interesting sights around here?'

'The trouble is,' people said, 'we don't know any Italian, but if you want to see something interesting, we've got a merry-go-round and swings, all sorts of concerts, a fancy restaurant, a zoo, and goodness knows what else.'

'Well, perhaps we'll try the merry-go-round and the swings first, and then a concert and the zoo,' said the macaronies.

'Well, in that case you go such and such a way,' people said, and the macaronies walked on and visited the merry-go-round and swings, and a concert, and the zoo.

It was all very interesting, but in the end the macaronies felt cold, their feet were frozen, and they said to one another, 'It was all very interesting. All macaronies ought to see things like that. But now let's go and sit down in a restaurant.'

So they went into a restaurant, sat down quietly, and chatted together in Italian. When the waiter heard them, he said to himself, *I know how to please them – I'll bring them Italian macaroni. They'll enjoy that!* And

that's just what he did – he brought them macaroni.

As you can imagine, it was a pleasant surprise for the macaronies – the ones sitting at the table as well as the ones lying on the plates – and they all said at once, 'What a coincidence! What are you doing here?'

'Well,' said the macaronies sitting on the chairs, 'we were bored stiff, so we went for a little walk and, because our feet were hurting us, we stopped off here.'

'Why didn't we think of that before now?' said the macaronies on the plates to one another. 'We might have seen something ourselves.'

'It's never too late. We've already seen all sorts of things. But you haven't seen any. Let's change places – you take our hats and raincoats, and we'll lie down on the plates. It's quite simple. Let's get on with it!'

So the macaronies that were lying on the plates jumped down on to the carpet. But the head waiter came running up and said to the ones at the table, 'Excuse me, I don't know any Italian, but what sort of manners have you got? All the macaroni is on the carpet, I thought you knew how to eat macaroni.' And he hurried away to fetch a dustpan and brush.

'Here are the hats and the raincoats,' said the first group of macaronies to the second. 'Get dressed while we get on to the plates.' And they climbed on to the plates, dipped their feet in the hot sauce, and felt fine.

When the head waiter arrived with the dustpan and brush, he saw that there were no macaronies on the carpet and that the guests were leaving. He was very surprised. 'Why are you leaving?' he wanted to know. 'Didn't you like the macaroni?'

'Excuse us,' said the macaronies who were about to leave, 'but how could we eat macaroni? Since when is genuine Italian macaroni eaten raw?'

The head waiter looked, and he saw that the macaronies on the plates really were raw. He made his apologies, thinking, 'What a disgrace!'

But the macaronies wearing hats and raincoats smiled and said, 'Never mind, that can easily happen.'

And they waved goodbye to the raw macaronies, and went out to have a look at the swings and the merry-go-rounds and at the whole world that is so very interesting.

Acknowledgements

The Estate of P. L. Travers for 'Chapter 3: Laughing Gas' from *Mary Poppins* copyright © P. L. Travers 1934, first published by Peter Davies Ltd in 1934; Michael Morpurgo for *Dolphin Boy* copyright © Michael Morpurgo 2004, first published by Anderson Press Ltd in 2004; 'The Great Mushroom Mistake' from *Uninvited Ghosts*, copyright © Penelope Lively, first published by William Heinemann Ltd; 'Vasilissa, Baba Yaga and the Little Doll' from *The Silent Playmate* copyright © Naomi Lewis, first published by Victor Gollancz Ltd; Richford Becklow Agency on behalf of Leila Berg for 'The Lory who Longed for Honey' from *The Nightingale and Other Stories* copyright © Leila Berg 1951, first published by Oxford University Press in 1951; Grace Hallworth and Octopus Publishing for 'How Fire Came to Earth' from *A Web of Stories* copyright © Grace Hallworth, first published by Methuen Children's Books; *Theseus and the Minotaur* retelling by Charles Kingsley; 'Patrick Comes to School' from *Chocolate Porridge and Other Stories* copyright © Margaret Mahy 1987, first published by J. M. Dent in 1987; 'The Rajah's Ears' from *The Kingfisher Book of Funny Stories* copyright © Michael

Rosen, first published by Kingfisher; 'Strange Animal' from *Children of Wax*, copyright © Alexander McCall Smith 1989, first published by Canongate in 1989; 'Vardiello' from *Tales Two* copyright © Geoffrey Summerfield 1992, first published by HarperCollins Young Lions in 1992; Miloš Macourek for 'The Macaronies Who Went for a Walk' translated by Marie Burg from *Pohadky*, published by Dilia.

The publishers gratefully acknowledge the above for permission to reproduce copyright material. While every effort has been made to trace the appropriate sources for the stories in this collection, in the event of an erroneous credit the publishers will be more than happy to make corrections in any reprint editions.

A classic collection of tales to tell children of about four, featuring beloved characters and lively stories, by Michael Bond, Jill Barklem and Anne Fine amongst others, chosen by children's book expert Julia Eccleshare.

Paddington Bear has a magical moment, the animals of Brambly Hedge are struggling at Dusty's mill, Lara's godmother sorts out a noisy lion and Rapunzel is rescued from the tower . . .

A classic collection of tales for young readers of about five, featuring beloved characters and lively stories by Michael Bond, Jill Barklem, Elizabeth Laird and others, chosen by children's book expert Julia Eccleshare.

Paddington Bear tries to buy a birthday present, the animals of Brambly Hedge set off to the seaside, a greedy queen insists on having the biggest tree in the world and will Cinderella get to go to the ball?

A classic collection of tales for young readers
of about six, featuring beloved characters and
lively stories by P. L. Travers, Jill Barklem,
Michael Morpurgo and others, chosen by
children's book expert Julia Eccleshare.

The Banks family are searching for a nanny,
Macaw the parrot helps out at the fish and
chip shop and a stonecutter dreams of
becoming an emperor . . .

A classic collection of stories by Michael Rosen, Alexander McCall Smith, Ted Hughes, Michael Morpurgo and others, specially chosen for young readers of around eight by children's book expert Julia Eccleshare.

Mary Poppins takes Jane and Michael on a topsy-turvy day, a boy watches over a beautiful swan and more . . .